Back to School

RACHEL YODER—
Always Trouble Somewhere

Book 2

WANDA ✺
BRUNSTETTER

BARBOUR
PUBLISHING

Cover Artist: Richard Hoit

For more information about Wanda E. Brunstetter, please access the author's Web site at the following Internet address: www.wandabrunstetter.com

Published by Barbour Publishing, Inc., P.O. Box 719, Uhrichsville, Ohio 44683, www.barbourbooks.com

Our mission is to publish and distribute inspirational products offering exceptional value and biblical encouragement to the masses.

ecpa Member of the
Evangelical Christian
Publishers Association

Printed in the United States of America.

Dedication

To my daughter, Lorine, a *wunderbaar* schoolteacher.
And to my granddaughters, Jinell, Madolynne,
and Rebekah, who enjoy doing many fun things
at their country school.

Other books by Wanda E. Brunstetter

Fiction

Rachel Yoder Series
School's Out!—Book 1

Sisters of Holmes County Series
A Sister's Secret

Daughters of Lancaster County Series
The Storekeeper's Daughter
The Quilter's Daughter
The Bishop's Daughter

Brides of Lancaster County Series
A Merry Heart
Looking for a Miracle
Plain and Fancy
The Hope Chest

Nonfiction

Wanda Brunstetter's Amish Friends Cookbook
The Simple Life

Glossary

ab im kopp—go crazy
ach—oh
aldi—girlfriend
baremlich—terrible
bauchweh—stomachache
bensel—silly child
bletsching—spanking
boppli—baby
bopplin—babies
bruder—brother
daed—dad
daer—door
danki—thank you
dummkopp—dunce
dummle—hurry
ekelhaft—disgusting
fingerneggel—fingernails
galgedieb—scoundrel
grank—sick
kapp—cap
kinner—children
jah—yes
mamm—mom
maus—mouse
meis—mice
Mondaag—Monday
naerfich—nervous
nixnutzich—naughty

pescht—pest
rutschich—squirming
schnell—quickly
schtinkich—smelly
sei—hogs
uffgschafft—excited
wunderbaar—wonderful

Gern gschehne.   You are welcome.
Guder mariye.   Good morning.
Raus mit!   Out with it!
Sis mir iwwel.   I am sick at my stomach.
Was in der welt?   What in all the world?
Wie geht's?   How are you?

Contents

Chapter 1

First-Day Troubles

"Where's my sneaker? I can't find my other sneaker!" Rachel Yoder glanced down at her feet. On her left foot she wore a black and white sneaker, but her right foot was bare. *I can't go to school with only one shoe!*

Rachel dropped to her knees and peered under the sofa. No sneaker there; just a red checker piece from Pap's favorite game.

She crawled across the room to Mom's rocking chair and peeked underneath. Nope. Just the ball of blue yarn Rachel sometimes used when she played with her kitten, Cuddles. *Where could that sneaker be?*

Rachel had found one sneaker by her bed when she'd gotten up but couldn't find the other sneaker in her room. She grunted. "If that sneaker's not upstairs in my bedroom and it isn't down here in the living room, then where is it?"

She snapped her fingers. Maybe someone had hidden her sneaker so Rachel would be late for the first day of school. That wasn't something Henry, her sixteen-year-old brother, would do. But Jacob, who was almost twelve and liked to tease, might have taken it.

Rachel scrambled to her feet, stubbing her bare toe on the rocking chair. "Ouch! Ouch! Ouch!"

Hopping on one foot, she limped to the stairs and hollered, "Jacob Yoder! Did you take my sneaker?"

Jacob peeked around the banister at the top of the stairs and wrinkled his nose. "What would I want with your *schtinkich* old sneaker?"

"It is *not* smelly!" Rachel frowned. "And I can't go to school today with only one shoe on my foot."

Rachel's mother poked her head through the kitchen doorway. "Then you'd better plan to go barefooted, because if you and Jacob don't leave soon, you'll be late for the first day of school."

"Not if I ride my skateboard. Then I can get there in half the time."

As Mom stepped into the hallway, her silver-framed glasses slipped to the end of her nose. "No skateboard, Rachel! It's much too dangerous for you to ride that thing to school."

"I'll stay on the shoulder of the road, I promise."

Mom shook her head. "Absolutely not. You and Jacob will walk to school, same as you've always done—with or without your shoes."

Rachel stared down at her feet, her right foot bare with the aching toe, and the left foot clad in a black and white sneaker.

This isn't good. Not good at all. She wished she had asked for a bicycle for her birthday instead of a skateboard. But she was sure her parents would have said no. Rachel had seen English children ride bikes to school, but none of the Amish *kinner* she knew owned bikes. Even if she did own a bike, Mom probably wouldn't let her ride it to school.

Mom, and everyone else in the family, treats me like a boppli, Rachel thought.

"If you can't find your other sneaker, why don't you wear your church shoes?" Jacob suggested as he tromped down the stairs in new black boots Pap had bought him.

Rachel looked at her mother.

"*Jah*, sure," Mom said with a nod. "Hurry to your room and put them on. Be sure to fix your *kapp*, too, because it's on crooked," she called as Rachel dashed up the stairs.

"Always trouble somewhere," Rachel mumbled, straightening the small white covering perched on her head.

Rachel hurried to her bedroom closet. She usually kept her black leather church shoes on a wooden bench underneath her dresses. She bent to get them and discovered they both were missing.

Rachel blinked and scratched the side of her head. "*Was in der welt?* Now where have my church shoes gone?"

Rachel looked around the closet but only found a box of small rocks she planned to paint so they looked like ladybugs, a stack of games and puzzles, and the wooden skateboard Jacob and Henry had made for her birthday. She gazed at the skateboard longingly, wishing she could ride it to school.

With a frustrated sigh, Rachel ran to her bed. She dropped to her knees and peered underneath, but no church shoes were under her bed. She just saw the same dust balls she'd seen when she'd looked for her sneaker, and an old faceless doll with one missing arm.

Rachel clambered to her feet and raced to her dresser. She pulled open each drawer and rummaged through the sweaters, socks, and underwear. No sneaker or church shoes there, either.

"I don't need this kind of trouble," Rachel wailed as she banged the bottom drawer shut.

"Rachel! Jacob's ready to leave for school, so you'd better hurry," Mom called from downstairs.

"I can't find my church shoes!" Rachel shouted in return.

"Then you'd best go barefooted."

Rachel sucked in her lower lip. She couldn't walk to school in her bare feet. Her toe still hurt from where she'd stubbed it. Besides, too many pebbles lined the shoulder of the road between their house and the one-room schoolhouse. She thumped the side of her head. "Think, Rachel. Where did you put your shoes last Sunday after church?"

She took a seat on the edge of the bed and closed her eyes. *Let's see now. . .* She remembered coming to her room to change out of her Sunday dress. Then she'd taken off her shoes and—

Rachel jumped up and raced out of the room. "I know where my church shoes are!" she hollered, taking the stairs two at a time.

"You'd better slow down or you'll slip and fall," Mom scolded, shaking her finger at Rachel.

"You said I'd be late for school if I didn't hurry. I know where my church shoes are, so I need to get them right now!" Rachel hurried past Mom and nearly bumped into Jacob, who had just stepped out of the kitchen with his lunchbox in his hand.

"I'm heading out now, so if you're not ready to go, then you can walk by yourself," he said with a frown.

She placed her hands on her hips and scowled. "Go ahead. I don't need you to walk with me anyway!"

"I would prefer that you walk together," Mom said as she joined them near the back door. "There's safety in numbers, you know."

Jacob tapped the toe of his boot against the hardwood floor. "Then hurry up, Rachel. Time's a-wasting."

"I need my church shoes. I remember putting them in the utility room last Sunday so I wouldn't forget to polish them before our next preaching service." Rachel darted into the utility room and halted in front of Pap's wooden shoe-shining box. There sat one of her good shoes—but only one. The other one was not there.

"Oh, no," she groaned. "Not another missing shoe."

Rachel grabbed the shoe and ran back to her brother. "Jacob, did you take one of my church shoes?"

"Right." He snickered. "Like I would want one of your schtinkich shoes."

"My shoes are not smelly, and if you're playing a trick on me—"

Mom held up her hand to quiet Rachel and then faced Jacob. "Do you have your sister's church shoe?"

He shook his head. "'Course not. Why would I take her dumb old shoe?"

"You don't have time to look for it now," Mom said, glancing at the battery-operated clock on the wall. "Rachel, it looks like you have no choice but to go to school in your bare feet today."

"I've got a better idea." Rachel dropped to the floor, slipped the church shoe on her right foot, and stood. "Now I have one shoe on each foot."

Mom clicked her tongue against the roof of her mouth. "But the shoes don't match, Rachel."

"I don't care. At least my feet won't hurt on the walk to school."

Jacob nudged Rachel's arm with his elbow. "You're such a *bensel*."

She pushed his elbow away and grabbed her lunchbox from the counter. "I am not a silly child!"

"Think what you like, but don't complain to me if the kinner at school make fun of you today." Jacob snickered and headed out the door. "Everyone will probably think you're a little *bensel*."

Rachel figured Jacob would probably say things to irritate her all the way to school; but to her surprise, he walked a few feet ahead of her and never said a word. That was fine with Rachel. She'd rather daydream than talk to her brother anyway.

As Rachel continued to walk toward the Amish schoolhouse, her mind wandered. She thought about the skateboard she wished she could ride to school. She pictured Cuddles, her sweet little kitten, and thought about how much fun they had playing together. Then Rachel spotted a fancy red car speeding down the road, and she thought about how wonderful it would feel to go for a ride in a fast-moving car with the top down. Rachel figured she'd probably never get to ride in a convertible, but it was fun to think about sitting in the passenger's seat with the wind blowing the ties on her kapp, and her stomach jiggling up and down as the car bounced over the bumps in the road.

By the time Rachel and Jacob arrived at the schoolhouse, she'd forgotten all about her missing shoes—until a dark-haired Amish boy who looked to be about her age stepped onto the porch at the same time she did and pointed to her feet. "Say, how come you're wearing two different shoes?"

Rachel frowned. She didn't even know this boy, so why should she answer his question? Besides, he smelled funny—kind of like the fresh cloves of garlic Mom used when she made savory stew.

"Who are you?" she asked, sucking in her breath as she stepped backward.

He smiled, revealing deep dimples in his cheeks. "I'm Orlie Troyer. My family moved here from Indiana last week. What's your name? And why are you wearing shoes that don't match?"

"My name's Rachel Yoder." She stared at her feet. "I couldn't find both of my sneakers this morning, and I could only find one church shoe, so I wore one of each."

Orlie snickered. "Only a bensel would wear two different shoes."

Rachel stared into Orlie's chocolate-colored eyes and gritted her teeth. "I am not a silly child, and I can wear whatever shoes I want!" She released her breath in one long puff of air and took another step back.

"Ha! I say anyone who wears shoes that don't match has to be a bensel," he taunted.

Rachel gripped the handle of her lunchbox so hard, her fingers numbed. It was bad enough that she'd had to put up with Jacob's teasing. She didn't need anyone else bothering her today.

Orlie shifted from one foot to the other and stared at Rachel with a big grin on his face. It made her feel like a fly caught in a spider's web. "How old are you, Rachel?" he asked.

"I turned ten this summer."

His smile widened. "I turned ten last February."

"That's nice." Rachel tried to push past Orlie,

but he stood with his arms folded and his legs slightly spread, blocking the schoolhouse door.

"Are you in a hurry to get inside?" he asked in a teasing tone.

"As a matter of fact, I am."

"Not me. I don't like school so much." He wrinkled his nose. "Fact is, I'll be glad when I graduate eighth grade and can work for my *daed* in the blacksmith shop he's planning to open soon."

Rachel grunted. Orlie was short and thin. She didn't think he would have enough strength to do the hard work of a blacksmith, but she kept her opinion to herself.

When Orlie finally stepped away from the door, Rachel pushed past him. But *bam!* She tripped on a loose shoelace and fell flat on her face.

"Ugh!" She pulled herself to her feet, feeling the heat of embarrassment flood her cheeks.

Orlie held his sides and howled. "That's what happens when you don't tie your shoes. Maybe you should have come to school in your bare feet!"

Rachel jerked open the schoolhouse door.

Hope I don't have to sit near him today! she thought, glowering.

The schoolteacher, Elizabeth Miller, greeted Rachel inside the door. "*Guder mariye*, Rachel." When Elizabeth smiled, her blue eyes twinkled like fireflies.

"Good morning." Rachel was glad to have such a kind young woman as her schoolteacher. Elizabeth was a pretty woman with golden hair. She'd taught at the Amish one-room schoolhouse for two years, and Rachel had never heard her say an unkind word to any pupils, whom the Amish referred to as "scholars."

Soon everyone was sitting behind desks. Rachel knew Elizabeth might rearrange the seats, but for now, she was happy to be seated at a desk across the aisle from her cousin Mary.

"How come you're wearing two different shoes?" Mary whispered, pointing at Rachel's feet.

Rachel grimaced. She was beginning to think wearing the mismatched shoes was a bad idea. "I'll tell you later."

Teacher Elizabeth tapped her desk with a ruler, and everyone got quiet. "Good morning, boys and girls."

"Good morning, Elizabeth," the scholars said in unison.

"We have a new boy in our school this year.

His name is Orlie Troyer. He recently moved here to Pennsylvania from the state of Indiana." The teacher smiled at Orlie. "I hope everyone will make him feel welcome."

All heads turned toward Orlie, whom Rachel soon discovered had taken a seat at the desk directly behind her. Orlie grinned and nodded at Rachel. She turned back around. *I hope Teacher moves that fellow to a different desk.*

Elizabeth opened her Bible and read from 1 Corinthians 13:11: " 'When I was a child, I talked like a child, I thought like a child, I reasoned like a child.' "

Rachel cringed. Jacob thought she was a silly child for wearing mismatched shoes, and so did Orlie. Did God think she was a silly child, too?

She shook her head. No, she knew she was a child of the King, and that meant she wasn't silly in God's eyes.

After the scripture reading, the scholars stood by their desks and repeated the Lord's Prayer. After the prayer, everyone filed to the front of the room and stood in rows according to their ages. Then they sang a few songs in German, the language Amish children spoke at home. Orlie, who was in the third grade, just like Rachel, had somehow managed to stand right beside her. He kept staring at her, and every time he opened his mouth, the smell of garlic drifted to Rachel's nose.

Rachel leaned away, but Orlie moved closer. Was he trying to pester her? Did he dislike her so much that he wanted to make her miserable?

Rachel was relieved when the singing time was over and she could return to her seat. At least with Orlie sitting behind her, she couldn't smell his breath so much.

Teacher Elizabeth wrote the math lessons for grades three to eight on the blackboard. Then she and her sixteen-year-old helper, Sharon Smucker, worked with the first and second graders, who needed to learn the English language better. When the clock on the wall behind the teacher's desk said ten o'clock, Elizabeth dismissed the scholars for morning recess.

Eager to be outside and away from Orlie, Rachel hurried to the swings with Mary.

"That new boy is sure a *pescht*," Rachel said, glancing over at Orlie, who stood across the schoolyard, talking to Jacob and some of the other boys. She bit off a piece of her fingernail and spit it to the ground.

Mary wrinkled her nose. "That's so gross. Why do you have to do that to your *fingerneggel*, Rachel?"

"I only chew my fingernails when I'm nervous or upset. That Orlie has me upset," Rachel explained.

"So, why do you think Orlie's a pest?" Mary asked.

"He made fun of me because I'm wearing two different shoes."

Mary giggled and pointed to Rachel's feet. "That is pretty strange."

"Can I help it if I couldn't find matching shoes this morning?" When Rachel looked across the yard, she noticed that Orlie was staring at her instead of talking to the other boys. "He's doing it again."

"Doing what?"

"He's staring at me, just like he was doing before school started."

"Maybe he likes you."

"He doesn't even know me." Rachel shrugged. "Besides, I don't like him."

"Why not?"

"Because he likes to tease and stare at me."

Rachel wrinkled her nose and made a choking sound. "He smells like garlic, too."

Mary nudged Rachel's elbow. "Didn't you hear what the bishop said during church last Sunday?"

"What was that?" Rachel had been daydreaming during part of the service and had missed hearing most of the bishop's sermon, so she wasn't sure what Mary meant.

"He said we're supposed to love everyone. Even those who are dirty or smell bad."

"That's easy for you to say. You didn't have to stand beside Orlie during singing. He's not sitting behind you, either." Rachel grabbed the chain on her swing, pushed off with one foot, and spun around until the ground began to whirl. "I'm flying," she hollered, leaning her head way back. "I feel like a bird soaring up in the sky."

"The ties on your kapp are flying, too," Mary said. "If you're not careful, you'll lose it."

Rachel ignored her cousin and continued to spin. But suddenly, her stomach churned. She climbed off the swing as the teacher called them inside, and she could barely stand.

Rachel took a couple of shaky steps, stumbled backward, and held her stomach. "*Ach*, I don't feel so good."

"What's wrong?" Mary asked, reaching for Rachel's hand.

Rachel pulled back. "I—I think I'm gonna be sick." She turned and dashed for the outhouse.

When Rachel stepped out of the outhouse several minutes later, Orlie stood right outside the door, as though he'd been waiting for her. "Your face looks kind of green, Rachel. Are you *grank*?"

Rachel clenched her fingers so hard they ached. "I'm not sick. Just got dizzy from too much twirling on the swings, and I—I lost my breakfast."

"You should know better than to spin like that, little bensel," Orlie said, shaking his head. "Didn't your *mamm* teach you anything?"

"My mom's taught me plenty, and I am *not* a silly child!"

"My mom's taught me plenty, and I am *not* a silly child," Orlie repeated with a grin.

"It's not polite to mimic," she said.

Orlie shook his head. "It's not polite to mimic."

"Then stop doing it."

"Then stop doing it."

Rachel was tempted to say something more,

but she figured Orlie would just copy her if she did. So she hurried to the schoolhouse and took a seat behind her desk. This day couldn't be over soon enough as far as she was concerned. She'd had enough first-day troubles!

Chapter 2

Lunchbox Surprise

"I don't feel like going to school today. Can I please stay home?" Rachel asked her mother when she entered the kitchen the following morning.

Mom turned from the stove, where she was frying bacon. "Are you grank?"

Rachel shook her head. "I'm not sick, but I—"

"If you're not grank, then you'll go to school, same as always."

"But, Mom, Orlie will be there, and he'll probably tease me again."

"Who's Orlie?"

"He's a new boy at school. His family moved here from Indiana," Jacob said as he came into the kitchen.

"I see. Son, have you finished your chores?"

Mom asked, turning back to the stove.

"Jah, but Henry and Pap are still doing theirs, and Esther's milking the cows. Pap said to tell you they'd be in for breakfast in about ten minutes." Jacob hung his straw hat on a wall peg near the door and went to the sink to wash his hands.

"The bacon and eggs should be done by then, so that will work out fine and dandy," Mom called over her shoulder.

Rachel sighed. Didn't anyone care about her problem with Orlie?

Mom looked at Jacob. "Would you please set some juice out?"

Jacob pointed to himself. "Who, me?"

She nodded. "Jah, I was talking to you."

"Okay." He dried his hands on a towel and headed to the refrigerator.

Mom nodded at Rachel. "I'd like you to set the table."

"I was just about to." Rachel pulled a stool to the cupboard. Then she climbed up and removed six plates and six glasses, which she placed on the counter. As she opened the silverware drawer, she decided to bring up the subject of Orlie Troyer again. "Orlie made fun of me yesterday, just because I was wearing two different shoes."

"Well, you can wear matching ones today," Mom said, "since soon after you left for school yesterday I found both of your shoes out in the barn. I figure that mischievous cat of yours must have hauled them there, because I discovered her playing with the sneaker."

Rachel frowned. She knew Mom didn't like Cuddles to be in the house, and now that she thought the cat had taken Rachel's shoes, Rachel hoped Mom wouldn't say Cuddles couldn't come inside anymore.

"I don't think Cuddles could have taken them," Rachel said. "She's just a kitten. I don't think she's strong enough. And I think they're too big for her to carry."

"That cat is big for a kitten, though," Mom pointed out. "She might have dragged the shoes out there by the laces."

"Even if it was Cuddles, she didn't hurt my shoes," Rachel said. "She probably wanted something of mine to keep her company."

"Puh!" Mom waved the spatula like she was batting a fly. "That cat's been nothing but trouble since the Millers gave her to you."

Rachel didn't think her kitten had been a bit

of trouble. In her opinion, Cuddles was a nice little kitten, who had kept Rachel company and helped her not to feel so scared when she'd been locked in their neighbor's cellar. But there was no use saying all that to Mom. What really mattered was how Rachel was going to get out of going to school.

She hurried to put the dishes, glasses, and silverware on the table, then moved over beside her mother. "I'm done setting the table now. Do you need my help with anything else?"

"You can scramble some eggs while Jacob pours the juice."

Jacob grunted. "I think I should have stayed in the barn and helped Pap and Henry with their chores."

Mom squinted her blue eyes as she glared at Jacob. "What was that?"

"Nothing, Mom," Jacob mumbled. He picked up the pitcher of juice and poured some into the first glass, while Rachel went to the refrigerator and took out a carton of eggs. She'd just finished mixing them in a bowl, when she decided to bring up the subject of Orlie again.

"Orlie teased me when I threw up after twirling on the swings yesterday. He mimicked me, too, and kept staring and whispering to me all day."

"He probably has a crush on you, sister," Jacob said before Mom could respond. "Boys tease when they're trying to impress a girl."

"He doesn't have a crush on me, and he certainly doesn't impress me!" Rachel's forehead wrinkled, and she fought the urge to bite a fingernail. "I don't like him much, either."

"That's not nice to say, Rachel," Mom said with a click of her tongue. "If you give the boy a chance, you might find that he's quite likeable."

"I doubt it," Rachel said with a huff. "Besides, Orlie's a pescht, and his breath smells funny— like he gargled with garlic juice."

Mom's glasses slipped to the end of her nose as she pursed her lips. "The Bible says we are to love everyone, Rachel."

"It's hard to love someone who's making your life miserable."

"God wants us to love even our enemies."

"I could like Orlie better if he didn't tease me, stare at me, or smell like garlic." As though Rachel's fingers had a mind of their own, one of them slipped right between her teeth.

"No nail biting, Rachel," Mom scolded.

"Biting your nails is a disgusting habit," Jacob put in.

Rachel pulled her finger out of her mouth and held her hands tightly against her sides. She felt more nervous today than any other time she could remember. She dreaded what Orlie might do to tease her. She'd always liked going to school—until Orlie Troyer had come and ruined it all.

"Can't I stay home from school just this once?" she begged, ignoring Jacob's nail-biting comment. He was no better than Orlie Troyer. Jacob just wanted to upset her.

Mom shook her head so hard the ties on her kapp swished from side to side. "You may stay home only when you're sick. Is that clear?"

Rachel nodded and sighed deeply as she reached for the stack of napkins in the center of the table. She realized she wouldn't get her way on this, so she could only hope and pray that Orlie wouldn't bother her again today.

When Rachel entered the schoolyard with Jacob later that morning, she noticed Mary playing on one of the teeter-totters with some other girls. Rachel was about to join Mary, when Orlie stepped out from behind a bush, blocking her path. "I see you're wearing matching sneakers today," he said, smirking and pointing at her feet.

She merely shrugged and fought the temptation to plug her nose as the strong aroma of garlic greeted her yet again.

Orlie stared at her with a peculiar look on his face, and Rachel felt like a bug about to be squashed. "Can I ask you something, Orlie?" she questioned.

He nodded. "Jah, sure. Ask me anything you like."

"What did you have for breakfast this morning?"

"Eggs, sausage, and biscuits. Why?"

Rachel fidgeted with the ties on her kapp as she shifted her weight from one foot to the other. Should she ask why his breath smelled so bad, or would that make him tease her more? "Well, I was wondering—"

"Well, I was wondering—" Orlie mimicked. He tipped his head to one side, and a chunk of dark hair fell across his forehead. "What were you wondering, Rachel?"

She drew in a deep breath. "Did you have anything with garlic on it?"

Orlie's face turned red as a pickled beet. "My mamm gives me a clove of garlic to eat every morning. She says it's to keep me from getting a cold." He shuffled his feet and glanced around as though he were worried someone might hear. "When we lived in Indiana, I got sick a lot and missed many days of school. Mom didn't want me to miss school this year."

Rachel stifled a giggle. She figured the garlic remedy probably worked pretty well, because with breath that bad, nobody would want to get close to Orlie. So he sure couldn't get any cold germs from anyone!

"You're not gonna tell anyone I eat a hunk of garlic for breakfast every day, are you?"

Rachel shook her head. No need for that. Anyone coming near Orlie would know he'd eaten a good dose of garlic. No wonder Pap called garlic "the stinking rose." Phew! She could hardly stand the disgusting odor.

The school bell rang, and Rachel felt a sense of relief. With Orlie sitting behind her, she wasn't close enough to him to smell his horrid breath. Unless she turned around, of course, which she had no intention of doing on purpose.

"Good morning, boys and girls," Rachel's

teacher said with a smile as the scholars took their seats.

"Good morning, Elizabeth," the children said in unison.

Elizabeth opened her Bible. "Today I'll be reading from Mark 12:30 and 31. 'Love the Lord your God with all your heart and with all your soul and with all your mind and with all your strength. The second is this: "Love your neighbor as yourself." There is no commandment greater than these.' "

Rachel reflected on those verses. She thought loving God with her whole heart, soul, mind, and strength was easy enough, because God was a loving God who cared for His people and deserved everyone's love in return. Loving her neighbors wasn't too hard, either, since Rachel liked most of the folks who lived near them.

Then she thought of Orlie and frowned. Orlie wasn't so easy to love, however; but maybe she didn't have to, since he wasn't a close neighbor. Of course, Mom had reminded her this morning that the Bible said everyone should love even their enemies. Orlie wasn't exactly an enemy. So, if he wasn't Rachel's neighbor and he wasn't her enemy, maybe she didn't have to love him at all.

Maybe the best thing to do was to pretend Orlie didn't exist. Yes, that's what she would do.

Rachel felt someone tap her on the shoulder. "*Psst. . .*Rachel, didn't you hear the teacher?"

Rachel sat there, determined to ignore Orlie.

Tap. Tap. He thumped harder this time.

Rachel whirled around. "What do you want?"

"It's time to stand and recite the Lord's Prayer."

Rachel turned back around and realized everyone else in the room was standing—and staring at her! She quickly jumped to her feet. So much for her plan to ignore Orlie Troyer.

The rest of the morning went fairly well, but at noon, when Rachel sat on the porch to eat her lunch, she discovered an unwanted surprise. Inside her lunchbox was a tuna fish sandwich with a hunk of wilted lettuce.

"Yuck! I don't like tuna," Rachel moaned. She thought tuna was disgusting, and it made her feel funny bowing her head to say a silent prayer of thanks for something she wasn't even thankful to eat. She closed her eyes. "Please God, no more tuna," she whispered out loud to let Him know how serious she was.

Orlie plopped down beside Rachel and tapped

her on the shoulder just as she finished praying. "What'd you say?"

She grunted and slid to the edge of the porch, hoping he would take the hint and find somewhere else to sit. "Nothing."

"Yes, you did. You said something about tuna."

Rachel figured she may as well tell Orlie what she was upset about or he'd probably keep bothering her. "I asked my mamm for a peanut butter and jelly sandwich today, and she gave me tuna instead."

His eyebrows lifted a little. "You don't like tuna?"

"No way! It's oily and fishy and tastes really gross."

"No way! It's oily and fishy and tastes really gross."

Rachel ground her teeth together and stared at him. "Stop mimicking me."

"I like tuna just fine. For that matter, there's not much I don't like in the way of food," Orlie said with a nod.

Rachel didn't comment on Orlie's last statement; she just sat there trying to think of what to do with the disappointing sandwich she held in her hand and wishing Orlie would sit with the boys out on the lawn.

"'Course there's some things not related to food that I don't like," Orlie continued. "Want to know what they are?"

"Not really. Why don't you just eat your lunch and leave me alone?"

"I don't like buzzing bees, stinky pigs, dogs that bite, or smelly cow manure," he said, as if he hadn't heard Rachel's request. "And I don't care much for dirty little mice, either."

Rachel rolled her eyes skyward. Then she glanced around to make sure no one was watching. She was in luck. Everyone seemed busy eating their own lunches, and no one was looking Rachel's way. Since Teacher Elizabeth had brought her lunch outside and was sitting on a quilt under the maple tree, Rachel figured she could sneak back into the schoolhouse unnoticed. She grabbed the sandwich, hurried across the porch, pulled open the door, and dashed to the garbage can. With only a slight hesitation, she dropped the sandwich in and headed back outside to finish eating her lunch.

Since Orlie was still sitting on the porch, Rachel decided to take her lunchbox and sit on the grass near Mary. Unfortunately, Orlie followed and flopped down beside her. She looked the other way, and her stomach rumbled as she stared at her lunchbox. She only had a thermos of milk and one apple left. At this rate, she would starve to death before supper time.

"Want half of my sandwich?" Orlie offered. "It's bologna and cheese."

"No thanks," she said with a shake of her head. No way was she going to eat anything of Orlie's. It might have garlic on it.

Chapter 3

Dinky

"I'm sure glad this is Saturday and there's no school," Rachel said as she climbed the stairs from the basement and followed her sister into the kitchen. Pap, Henry, and Jacob were working in the fields, and Mom had gone to Grandpa and Grandma Yoder's place soon after breakfast to help Grandma clean her house.

Esther set down the wooden box she'd brought up from the basement and turned to face Rachel. "You don't like school this year? You've always liked it before."

"I like school just fine. I *don't* like Orlie Troyer."

"He's that new boy at school, right?"

"Right. And Orlie's a real pain—always teasing, staring at me, mimicking things I say,

and blowing his garlic breath right in my face."
Rachel wrinkled her nose and tapped the side
of her head. "It's enough to make me go *ab im
kopp.*"

Esther chuckled. "Oh, Rachel, how you do
exaggerate. I'm sure nothing that boy could ever
do or say would make you go crazy."

Rachel shrugged. Esther could think whatever
she wanted; she wasn't the one who had to put
up with Orlie's irritating behavior. "There's
another reason I don't like school this year."

"Oh? What's that?"

"I have to walk with Jacob every day, and he
complains because I walk too slow," Rachel said.
"I wish I could ride a bike to school, like some
English kinner get to do."

"Some folks believe other people's bread tastes
better than their own," Esther said.

Rachel nodded. "Mom has told me that more
than once."

"It's true. We shouldn't waste time wanting
things others own. We should be happy with
what we have."

Rachel tried to be satisfied, but sometimes it
wasn't so easy. "Even if Mom and Pap did let me
have a bike, Mom would probably say I'm too

young to ride it to school." She shook her head and groaned. "Why does everyone treat me like a baby?"

Esther patted Rachel's arm. "Being the youngest member of the family must be hard."

Rachel nodded. "If Mom had another boppli, I wouldn't be the baby of the family anymore. Maybe then Mom and Pap would realize I'm grown up and would let me do more things."

"Jah, maybe so, but since Mom hasn't had any *bopplin* since you were born, she probably won't have any now." Esther rubbed a spot on her lower back. "Whew! That box was heavier than I thought. Guess I should have asked Pap or one of the boys to haul it up from the basement for me before they headed out to the fields."

"I could have helped you with it," Rachel pointed out. Sometimes she felt her older sister treated her like a baby, too. Just because Rachel was only ten years old didn't mean she wasn't strong or couldn't help with certain things. At least she should be allowed to try.

"You can help me now." Esther motioned to the box sitting near her feet. "I want to check these good dishes over thoroughly for any cracks or chips; and then we need to wash them so they'll be ready in plenty of time for my wedding on the first Thursday of November."

Rachel sighed. November seemed like a long time off, especially since she had to go to school every day between now and then. And she had to face that teasing, smelly-breath Orlie Troyer.

"Are you sighing because you don't want to help me?" Esther asked, reaching for the box.

"Oh, no. I'm happy to help," Rachel was quick to say. "I was just thinking that your wedding seems like a long time from now. I wish it could get here sooner."

"It's only two months away, and we have a lot to do, so I'm sure the time will go quickly. If Mom hadn't gone to help Grandma clean her house this morning, she'd be here now, helping me." Esther smiled. "So I really appreciate your help, little sister."

Rachel pulled her shoulders back and stood as tall as she could. It was nice to be appreciated. "I'm sure I can do whatever Mom would have done."

"Jah, I'm sure you can." Esther dropped to her knees by the box. "Now first we open the box and take out the dishes."

"Okay." Rachel knelt beside her sister and

fought the urge to rip the box open herself. She knew it would be better to let Esther do that, since the dishes were Mom's best china and would be used at Esther and Rudy's wedding.

Esther's hands shook like leaves fluttering in the breeze as she slowly lifted the lid. "I'm so *uffgschafft* I can barely make my fingers work."

Rachel didn't see why her sister was so excited about opening a box of old dishes, but she didn't say anything. She didn't want to hurt Esther's feelings.

When Esther lifted the lid, Rachel saw a row of delicate white china cups with little pink roses. Esther smiled slightly as she removed each one and set it carefully on the floor by the box. The layer under the cups held plates, and when Esther reached inside to remove the first one, the shredded paper surrounding the dishes moved a little. At first, Rachel thought it shifted from the movement of the plate, but when a little gray blob with beady eyes poked its head out of the paper, she knew what had happened.

"Ach! It's a *maus*! It's a maus!" Esther hollered, jumping to her feet. "That's so *ekelhaft*!"

"It's not disgusting. It's only a baby mouse that must have found its way in through here."

Rachel pointed to a small hole in the side of box. She reached inside and picked up another plate, and the whole box seemed to move. Five little gray mice scurried about, ducking their heads in and out, and pushing shreds of paper in every direction.

Esther let out an ear-piercing screech and hopped onto the closest chair. Her eyes looked like they were ready to pop right out of her head, and her face was as white as a pail of goat's milk.

Rachel could hardly keep from laughing at her silly sister. "Want me to catch the mice and take them outside?" she asked.

"Jah, sure. If you think you can."

"Of course I can." Rachel had a way with animals, and she certainly wasn't afraid of a little old mouse, so she marched to the pantry and pulled out a paper sack. Then she hurried back to the box and reached inside. She felt brave and grown-up. One by one, she picked up the baby mice and placed them carefully into the sack.

"It's safe for you to get off that chair now," she said, trying not to smile at her sister's anxious expression.

Esther clung to the chair like she feared for her life. "H–how do you know there aren't more creepy mice inside that box?"

"Well, let me see." Rachel slipped her hand into the box again, while she hung on to the sack with the other hand. She dug around one side and then the other, dipping her fingers up and down and all through the shreds of paper. "Nothing is in here now except for more dishes."

One of Esther's brows rose to a jaunty angle. "Are—are you sure?"

"I'm very sure," Rachel replied with a nod. "But if you're scared, then you can wait until I come back to the house. Then we can take the rest of the dishes out together."

Esther lifted her chin and frowned at Rachel. "I am not scared. I just don't like mice. I especially don't like the idea of their dirty little feet climbing all over my good wedding dishes."

I just don't like mice. I just don't like mice. Rachel remembered hearing similar words the other day at school. But who had said them? Who had told her they didn't like mice? She squeezed her eyes shut and tried to remember, but nothing came to mind. Oh well, she guessed it wasn't important. She needed to get the baby mice outside so Esther could climb down from that chair.

"I'll be back soon," Rachel announced.

"Jah, okay."

As Rachel opened the back door and stepped onto the porch with the bag full of mice, for some reason an image of Orlie Troyer popped into her mind. Thanks to Orlie, Rachel didn't like going to school anymore, and that wasn't fair. Well, she wasn't one to give up easily. If she could find a way to get Orlie to quit bothering her, she would do it. If she could only find something Orlie didn't like and tease him with it, maybe he'd finally leave her alone.

The bag in Rachel's hand vibrated as the mice skittered inside.

"That's it!" she shouted. "Orlie's the one who said he didn't like mice!"

A smile spread across Rachel's face. She decided she would turn four of the baby mice loose in the field behind their house, but she had other plans for mouse number five.

Rachel trudged across the yard, climbed over the fence, stopped to pet the old horse Pap had put out to pasture, and headed for the cornfield. When she got there, she opened the sack and released four of the mice. "Good-bye little *meis*. Have a good life."

She crossed the pasture, gave old Tom another

pat, climbed over the fence, and headed for
the barn. There she found some coffee cans
in a cupboard under her father's workbench.
Pap liked to save the cans to store his nails and
other things. Rachel figured since her father had
several empty cans, he wouldn't miss just one.
She placed the paper sack that held the baby
mouse onto the workbench, then wadded up a
clean rag she'd found in one of the workbench
drawers and put it on the bottom of the can.
Then she took a screwdriver and poked a few
holes in the plastic lid of the can.

"All right, little maus, in you go." Rachel
opened the sack, removed the mouse, and placed
it inside the can. "This will be your new home
until Monday morning," she said with a satisfied
smile. "And from now on your name will be
Dinky."

The little gray mouse wiggled its whiskers at
her as she put the lid on the can.

Suddenly Cuddles scampered across the floor
and stopped at Rachel's feet. The kitten stared
at Rachel with sad eyes, meowing for all she was
worth.

Rachel felt bad because she hadn't spent much
time with Cuddles lately, so she sat on a bale of

hay, placed the coffee can beside her, and lifted
Cuddles into her arms. "Hey, there, sweet kitten,
have you missed me?"

Cuddles uttered a pathetic *meow*, then she
licked Rachel's nose with her sandpapery tongue.

Rachel giggled. "That tickles."

Cuddles snuggled against Rachel and began
to purr. Rachel closed her eyes. The kitten's
warm body and her purring felt so good that
Rachel knew she could easily fall asleep. She
opened her eyes, determined not to give in to
the sleepy feeling, and sat there stroking Cuddles
behind her ears.

Suddenly, Cuddles's nose twitched, and her
ears perked up. *Meow!* She leaped off Rachel's
lap and landed near the coffee can that held
Dinky captive.

"Oh no, you don't," Rachel scolded, when
Cuddles sniffed the lid of the can and swiped at
it. "That mouse is going to be my pet, and he's a
got a job to do at school on Monday morning."
She picked up the can and rushed out of the
barn.

Quickly, she made her way to the house and
slipped inside the front door, so Esther wouldn't
hear her from the kitchen. Then, as quietly as

she could, she tiptoed up the stairs and went straight to her room. She scurried to her bed, dropped to her knees, and slid the coffee can as far underneath the bed as she could. She'd give Dinky food later so he'd have plenty of energy for his mission on Monday morning.

Rachel glanced at the clock by her bed and realized she'd been gone quite awhile. Esther probably wondered what was taking her so long, so she needed to hurry and get back to the kitchen.

Esther stood at the sink, washing the wedding dishes. "What took you so long?" she asked. "I was beginning to wonder if you were ever coming back."

"Sorry. On my way out to the cornfield, I stopped to say hello to old Tom; and then on the way back to the house, I spent a few minutes in the barn with my kitten." Rachel wasn't about to tell her sister about Dinky. If Esther knew, she'd probably tell Mom and Pap about Rachel's plans.

Esther flicked a soapy bubble at Rachel. "I started washing the dishes without you."

Rachel grabbed a clean towel from the drawer near the sink and reached for a china cup. "I'm here now, so I'll dry the dishes."

Esther smiled. *"Danki."*

"You're welcome."

As Rachel dried each dish, she carefully set it on the counter. The last thing she wanted to do was to break one of Esther's wedding dishes. Mom would scold her for sure if that happened. Esther probably would, too.

When they finished with the dishes, Esther told Rachel, "I've been thinking. . ."

"What have you been thinking?"

"You mentioned earlier how much you dislike walking to school with Jacob."

Rachel nodded. "That's true."

"Why don't you see if Mom will let you wait at the end of our driveway until some of the other scholars go by? Then you can walk with them."

"I suppose I could, but Jacob would probably tag along, and he'd still badger me about walking too slow," Rachel answered. "Then the others would probably make fun of me, too."

Esther pulled Rachel to her side and hugged her. "I know it's hard being a child, but someday, when you're grown and married with kinner of your own, you'll realize your school days weren't so bad after all."

Rachel shook her head. "That won't happen, because I'm never getting married. Not ever!"

Chapter 4

A Hard Lesson

On Monday morning, after Rachel ate breakfast, she hurried to help Mom and Esther do the dishes; then she turned toward the stairs leading to her room.

"Where are you going, Rachel?" Mom called to her. "You don't want to be late for school."

"I just need to get something from my bedroom," Rachel explained. She scampered up the stairs before Mom could say anything else. When she entered her room a few seconds later, she rushed to her dresser and pulled open the bottom drawer. She took out a large matchbox with several tiny holes along the top. Next, she went over to her bed, got down on her hands and knees, and pulled out Dinky's coffee can.

Rachel opened the lid and lifted Dinky out by

his tail. Then she placed him in the matchbox. She couldn't hide a coffee can at school, but she knew she could easily hide a matchbox. Dinky looked happy and plump, because Rachel had taken good care of him, feeding him bits of cheese and cracker covered in peanut butter.

With a satisfied smile, Rachel rushed back to her dresser and grabbed a sweater from the same drawer where she'd hidden the matchbox. She wrapped the sweater around the matchbox, tucked it under her arm, and headed downstairs.

When Rachel entered the kitchen, she spotted Esther sweeping the floor. Mom stood at the counter, making a peanut butter and jelly sandwich. *At least it's not tuna this time,* thought Rachel.

"Jacob's outside waiting for you," Mom said. She slipped the sandwich into a plastic bag and placed it inside Rachel's lunchbox. Then she tipped her head to one side and stared at Rachel. "What's with the sweater this morning?"

"In case I get cold," Rachel said. She grabbed the lunchbox off the counter and ran to the door, hoping Mom wouldn't ask more questions.

"I don't see how you could possibly get cold," Esther said. "It's been so warm the last few days;

I can't imagine why you'd need a sweater."

Rachel shrugged. "That may be true, but fall is almost here. You never know when the weather might turn chilly."

Mom and Esther exchanged glances, but neither of them said a word. Rachel breathed a sigh of relief and hurried out the door.

Jacob stood on the porch, tapping his foot. "Well, it's about time. Are you trying to make us late for school?" he asked with a scowl.

She shook her head. "We won't be late, unless you dillydally."

"Jah, right. You're always the one who walks too slow. I don't stop to look at every bug and flower along the way like you do."

"Do not."

"Do so."

Rachel clamped her lips together so she wouldn't say anything more. She was in no mood to argue with Jacob. She only wanted to get Dinky safely to school so she could teach Orlie his first—and hopefully best—lesson of the day.

At school, Rachel slipped into the classroom while other children were still playing in the schoolyard. She was relieved to see that Teacher Elizabeth was busy writing something on the blackboard. Rachel tiptoed to Orlie's desk. She took the matchbox out of the folds of her sweater, lifted the lid on his desk, and placed it inside, where Orlie was sure to find it when he reached for his school supplies.

Rachel scooted out the front door and joined Mary on the swings.

"You're not going to throw up again, I hope," Mary said, wrinkling her nose, as her lips scrunched together.

Rachel shook her head. "I've learned my lesson about twirling on the swings."

"That's good to hear, because you looked green in the face when you came out of the outhouse that day, and I was worried about you."

"I've never gotten sick at school before," Rachel said. She pulled hard at the chains on the swing. "And I hope I never do again."

"Me neither. It's not fun to be grank."

"The only good part of being sick is that you get to stay home from school." Rachel pumped her legs to get the swing moving faster.

"Why would you want to stay home?" Mary asked. "Last year you liked school."

"That was true, until Orlie Troyer moved here and made my life so miserable."

Mary clicked her tongue, the way Mom often did. "He only bothers you because he knows he can."

"What's that mean?"

"It means, if you ignored him, he'd probably leave you alone. When a boy knows that his teasing bothers a girl, he does it more."

Rachel let her cousin's words roll around in her head awhile. Maybe Mary was right. If she didn't let Orlie know she was upset by the things he said and did, maybe he would leave her alone. "But it's too late for that," she mumbled when the school bell jangled. Orlie was about to get a big surprise.

Mary halted her swing. "Too late for what?"

"Oh, nothing." Rachel jumped off her swing. Then she hurried into the school. She knew if she was late, Orlie would probably tease her about that, too.

He deserves that little present I left him this morning! she thought. Finding a mouse in his desk might make him think twice about bothering her. And if that didn't work, she would ignore him, as Mary suggested.

Rachel glanced at Orlie as she passed his desk. He nodded and gave her a lopsided grin. She looked away quickly and slipped into her seat.

Teacher Elizabeth started the morning by

reading Luke 6:31. " 'Do to others as you would have them do to you.' "

Rachel's cheeks burned. Would she want someone to put something she was afraid of in her desk? No, of course not. A pang of regret shot through her. She gripped the sides of her desk, wishing she could run out the door. Maybe Orlie wouldn't see the matchbox. Then she could take it out of his desk during recess.

Rachel forced herself to stand beside her desk and recite the Lord's Prayer with the other scholars. But all she could think about was her naughty deed. She wondered if she'd get in much trouble.

A nudge in Rachel's back pushed her thoughts aside. "We're supposed to go up front so we can sing," Orlie said.

Rachel plodded to the front of the room with the others and moved her lips as though she were singing. *I wonder if Orlie will know I'm the one who put the mouse inside his desk.* She poked a fingernail between her teeth and nibbled until it broke. *He'll probably tell the teacher on me.*

After the singing, the scholars returned to their seats. Rachel's insides quivered as she sank into the chair behind her desk, fretting about what would happen when Orlie discovered the mouse.

Orlie passed Rachel's desk and wiggled his eyebrows. Rachel turned and watched as he flopped into his seat with a silly grin. He lifted the lid on his desk. Rachel's heart nearly stopped beating as she waited for him to see the matchbox she had placed there. But to her surprise, it wasn't a matchbox Orlie took out of the desk; it was his math book and some paper.

Maybe he didn't see the matchbox. Maybe I can still get it.

Rachel reached into her own desk to get her arithmetic book, but before she had a chance to open it, Teacher Elizabeth let out a shrill scream and hopped onto her chair.

"Ach! Ach! There's a maus on my desk!"

Rachel noticed the matchbox sitting on one corner of Teacher's desk. Why hadn't she noticed it before, and how did it get there?

Dinky poked his tiny head over a stack of papers. He darted around the desk a few times, hopped into the open drawer of Elizabeth's desk, jumped back out, and skittered down the side of the desk.

Thud! As Dinky landed on the floor, the room

filled with screams and screeches. A few girls leaped onto their chairs. Some boys sat at their desks, pointing at the mouse and laughing until tears ran down their cheeks. A few others joined Rachel in the chase to catch the mouse.

"Open the *daer* and maybe it'll run outside," Mary suggested.

"No, don't open that door!" Rachel hollered. She saw Dinky scurry under Mary's chair.

"If it comes my way I'll smash it," David Esh, the boy who sat in front of Mary, hollered.

"You'd better not kill my pet *maus*!" Rachel could have bitten her tongue. She hadn't meant to admit that Dinky was hers. Now everyone would think *she* had put the mouse on Teacher Elizabeth's desk.

Elizabeth stepped down from her chair just as Rachel scooped Dinky into her hands. "Rachel Yoder, is that your *maus*?"

Rachel nodded slowly. "Jah."

"Did you bring it to school to scare me?"

"No, Elizabeth."

"Then why was it in a matchbox? And why was it sitting on my desk?"

"Well, I—" Rachel shuffled her feet and stared at the floor.

"*Raus mit*—out with it!" Elizabeth's face was getting redder. Rachel knew she needed to say something to calm her teacher.

"I didn't bring Dinky—I mean the maus—to school to scare you, and I don't know how it got on your desk," she said.

"Well, it didn't get there by itself, now, did it?"

"No, Teacher."

"Put that mouse outside right now," Elizabeth demanded. "Then you'll need to sit down and do your math. You'll stay after school today to clean the chalkboard and do extra lessons."

Rachel felt sick. Dinky had become like a pet to her. If she let him go outside, she would never see him again. She didn't know how that matchbox got on Elizabeth's desk, but she figured Orlie must have had something to do with it. He'd probably found it in his desk and put it on the teacher's desk during the time of singing. Most likely he'd done it to get Rachel in trouble. Rachel disliked Orlie all the more. To make things worse, Jacob would have to stay late to walk her home. Then Mom and Pap would learn she'd taken a mouse to school, and that would spell trouble.

With a heavy heart, Rachel opened the

schoolhouse door, plodded down the steps, and set Dinky on the ground. "Good-bye, little friend. I hope you have a good, long life."

When Rachel returned to her seat, Orlie leaned over her shoulder and whispered, "Why you'd do it, Rachel? Why'd you put that maus in my desk?"

"You—you knew?"

"Jah, and I think it was a dirty trick."

Rachel sat with her arms folded. She could only think about losing Dinky and the punishment she'd get at home.

Guess that's what I get for trying to get even with Orlie, Rachel thought. *I should have just ignored him, like Mary said.*

Rachel decided to memorize Luke 6:31: "Do to others as you would have them do to you."

Chapter 5

Hurry-Up Cake

For the next several weeks, Rachel tried to stay out of trouble. She'd avoided Orlie so she wouldn't be tempted to do anything to him that she wouldn't want him to do to her. She also didn't want to do extra chores again. That had been her punishment for the mouse incident. She knew she'd been fortunate to escape a trip to the woodshed for a *bletsching*.

One Saturday morning Rachel looked at her calendar and realized it was Jacob's birthday.

"Oh, no," she moaned. "I forgot his birthday." Rachel and Jacob didn't always get along, but he was still her brother. She wanted to do something special to wish him a happy birthday.

Rachel rushed down the stairs and into

the kitchen. Seeing her mother in the room, she quickly stepped up to her and whispered, "Where's Jacob?"

"He's outside doing chores, along with your daed and older *bruder*." Mom nodded toward the basement door. "Esther went down to get the gift she hid for Jacob, and I asked her to bring up some canned peaches to go with our breakfast."

"I'm glad Jacob's not here."

Mom's glasses had slipped to the middle of her nose. She pushed them back in place and turned toward the stove. "Why are you whispering, Rachel?"

"I wanted to be sure Jacob didn't hear me."

"I just told you, he's outside doing chores."

Rachel felt the heat of embarrassment creep up the back of her neck. Mom must think she was hard of hearing, or a real *dummkopp*. "I just realized today's Jacob's birthday," she explained. "I don't have anything to give him, so I was hoping I could make something he might like to eat."

Mom opened the drawer at the bottom of the stove and reached for the frying pan. "Jacob has a sweet tooth, so why don't you bake him a cake?"

"Is there enough time?"

"There might be if you make a hurry-up cake.

That mixes and bakes faster than most other cakes."

"That's a great idea!" Rachel scurried to the cupboard where Mom kept baking supplies. "What exactly do I need?"

"Let's see now. . . The recipe calls for cake flour, baking powder, sugar, salt, vanilla, butter, milk, and eggs." Mom called out the ingredients so fast that Rachel could barely keep up. She rushed to the cupboard, then to the refrigerator to get everything she would need. She was tempted to ask her mother to repeat the list. But she didn't want Mom to think she was a little girl who couldn't remember anything.

"The directions for making the cake are in my recipe box," Mom said, as she plucked several brown eggs from the carton Rachel had just placed on the cupboard. "I'll need some of these for the French toast I'm making. That's one of Jacob's favorite breakfast foods."

Rachel nodded, even though she knew Jacob liked most food. He even liked tuna sandwiches and spinach, both of which Rachel could do nicely without.

"Be sure you mix the eggs and butter first. Then add the dry ingredients and milk alternately. Next, put in the vanilla and beat hard, and then pour the batter into two greased and floured cake pans. I'll heat the oven while you're doing that," Mom said.

Rachel's head felt as if it were spinning like a top. So much information rolled around. But she did her best to remember Mom's instructions. She was setting everything on the cupboard, when Esther entered the room. She had a large paper sack in one hand and a jar of peaches in the other hand.

"Where's the birthday boy?" she asked, handing Mom the peaches. Then she placed the sack on one end of the counter. "I figured Jacob would be in here looking for his birthday presents already."

"He's still doing chores with your daed and Henry." Mom motioned to Rachel. "Your sister's in a hurry to get a cake baked before Jacob comes in, so maybe you can help her."

Esther started toward Rachel, but Rachel shook her head. "If this is my gift to Jacob, then I need to make it myself," she explained.

"Okay, but let me know if you need anything." Esther opened one of the cupboard doors and removed a stack of plates. "I have to set the table anyway."

Rachel got out the recipe box and removed the card for hurry-up cake; then she quickly measured out the ingredients and put them in a large bowl. She hoped she hadn't forgotten anything, and that she'd put in the right amounts. The last thing she needed was for her cake to flop. Then Jacob and Henry would tease her.

"Watch out, Rachel, you're spilling flour all over the floor." Mom groaned. "I mopped in here after supper last night, and now you're making a mess."

"Sorry. I'll clean it up."

Rachel scurried to the utility closet to get the broom. She was on her way back when *phlumph!* She slipped in the spilled flour. The broom flew out of Rachel's hands, and she landed with a *thud* on the floor.

"Rachel, are you okay?" Mom and Esther asked at the same time. They hurried to Rachel's side.

"I'm all right." Rachel clambered to her feet, her face heating with embarrassment. Why was it that every time she tried to do something that might prove she was growing up, she made a mess of things?

"If you're going to finish Jacob's cake before he comes inside, you'd better get it in the oven and let me clean the floor," Esther said, bending to pick up the broom.

Rachel didn't argue. She hurried to the counter and poured the cake batter into two cake pans, while Esther swept the floor and Mom followed with a wet mop. Then Rachel carried the pans of cake batter across the room. She placed them in the oven. When that was done, she collapsed into the nearest chair. She didn't know how Mom and Esther did so much baking—mixing the hurry-up cake together made her tired. At least now, if Jacob came into the kitchen before the cake was done, she could tell him that his birthday present was in the oven.

"The table is set, Mom," Esther said a few minutes later. "What else would you like me to do?"

"You can open the jar of peaches and put it on the table."

"Okay." Esther tapped Rachel on the shoulder as she neared the table. "How are things at school these days? Are you getting along better with that new boy?"

Rachel wrinkled her nose. "School would be better for me if Orlie moved back to Indiana."

"Rachel," Mom scolded. "Orlie and his family

have as much right to live in Pennsylvania as we do."

"I wouldn't mind him being here so much if he didn't tease me, and if his breath smelled better."

"You don't mind the horses, and their breath doesn't always smell sweet," Esther said. She placed the jar of peaches on the table and opened the lid.

Rachel couldn't deny that fact. Just the other day, when she'd gone out to the pasture to visit old Tom, he'd blown his hot, smelly breath right in her face. "What you said about the horses' breath is true," she admitted, "but the horses—and none of our other animals—say mean things or stare at me in peculiar ways."

Mom set the frying pan on the gas stove and turned on the burner. "When I met Orlie and his folks at church, I thought he seemed like a nice boy."

Rachel folded her arms and frowned. "You don't know him like I do."

"Be that as it may, he's still a child of God, and you should be kind to him."

Rachel thought about the day she had tried to scare Orlie with the mouse. She wondered if her plan backfired because she'd been trying to get even. Maybe if she did something nice to Orlie for a change, he would leave her alone.

If any of Jacob's cake is left Monday morning, I'll take a piece to school for Orlie, she decided. *A hunk of yummy cake might sweeten Orlie's breath, too.*

Ding! Rachel jumped out of her chair when the timer on the stove sounded. "It's done! I've got to take Jacob's hurry-up cake out of the oven, let it cool, and frost it before he comes in."

Rachel grabbed two pot holders from a drawer near the stove. *Whoosh!* The heat roared at her as she opened the oven door. She carefully pulled out the cake pans. The cake layers looked a little browner than they should have. But they smelled good, and she thought that was a good sign. She walked carefully across the room and set the pans inside the refrigerator to cool them quicker. Then Rachel hurried to make strawberry icing.

By the time Rachel had mixed the icing, the cake pieces felt cool enough to frost. She took the cake out of the refrigerator. Still no Jacob. *He must not have finished his chores yet.* She picked up a cake pan and turned it upside down over a serving platter. It didn't budge. She tapped on the bottom of the pan with her hand. Nothing happened.

"Something's wrong with this cake," Rachel complained to her mother. "It won't come out of the pan."

"Try slipping a butter knife around the edges and see if that helps," Mom said.

Rachel did as her mother suggested, but the cake still wouldn't come loose. She tried the other pan. It wouldn't come out either. "Always trouble somewhere," she grumbled.

Esther stepped to Rachel's side. "Did you grease and flour the pans before you poured the batter in?"

Rachel squinted as she tried to remember what she had done. "Was I supposed to grease and flour them?"

"I told you to," Mom said. "When I gave you the instructions, I said to be sure you grease and flour the pans. It said so on the recipe card, too."

Rachel groaned. "I must have missed that part."

Just then, the back door opened, and Jacob stepped into the room, followed by Pap and Henry.

"Happy birthday, Jacob," Esther said, handing

him the paper sack she had set on the counter when she'd first come up from the basement.

"What's this?" Jacob asked, smiling at Esther.

Esther nudged his arm playfully. "It's your birthday present, silly."

Jacob's smile broadened as he peered in the sack. "Wow, a new baseball mitt! I've been hoping for one." He hugged Esther. "Danki, sister."

Esther smiled, and Rachel frowned. The hurry-up cake she'd made, that was stuck in the pans, was a stupid gift compared to what Esther had given Jacob. She wished she could hide the cake so Jacob wouldn't see it.

Pap went to the storage closet and opened the door. Then he pulled out a fishing pole and handed it to Jacob. "This is from your mamm and me."

Jacob set the mitt on the counter and cradled the fishing pole in his arms like a mother would hold her baby. "Danki, Pap. Danki, Mom. I've been wanting a new one of these, too."

"*Gern gschehne*—you are welcome," they said together.

"Now it's my turn," Henry announced. He pulled a wooden yo-yo from his jacket pocket and handed it to Jacob. "I made this for you. Happy birthday, bruder."

"It's real nice." Jacob rubbed his hand over the shiny wood, then he slipped the loop of string over his finger, flicked his wrist, and bounced the yo-yo up and down. "Works real well, too. Danki, Henry."

"Gern gschehne," Henry replied with a smile.

Everyone looked at Rachel as if waiting to see what she had for Jacob. She groaned and pointed to the cake pans sitting on the counter near the stove. "My present's over there, but sorry to say, I can't get either one of the cake layers out of their pans."

Jacob's eyebrows lifted high as he examined the cakes. "You baked me a cake?"

Rachel nodded. "I tried to, and since I wanted to get it done before you came in from doing your chores, I made a hurry-up cake. Only thing is, I got in such a hurry, I forgot to grease and flour the pans." Rachel motioned to the bowl of strawberry icing, and her chin trembled slightly. "Now I have a bowl of icing I can't use, two halves of a cake I can't get out of the pans, and nothing to give you for your birthday." She hoped she wasn't going to cry, because she figured Jacob would make a big deal out of it if she did.

However, instead of making fun of her cake mess, Jacob grabbed a knife from the silverware drawer. He scooped up a glob of strawberry icing and slathered it on half of the cake. "Nothin' says we can't eat it right out of the pan," he said, reaching back in the drawer for a fork.

Pap grabbed a fork, too, and so did Henry. Mom stopped them. "With a little help from my spatula, I'm sure I can get the cake layers out of their pans." She nodded at the stove. "I'm making Jacob's favorite this morning—French toast. So no cake until we've had our breakfast."

"Oh, all right," Jacob sighed, even though he was grinning. "I guess I can wait that long to sample some of Rachel's good-smelling cake." He thumped Rachel on the back. "Danki, sister. I appreciate it."

Rachel thought Jacob was only trying to make her feel better, but at least he hadn't said anything mean about her messed-up cake. Next year, she would try to remember to do something really special for his birthday. Maybe she would make him a painted rock. Rachel was pretty good at painting rocks to look like various animals, even if she did say so herself. At least those didn't have to be mixed, baked, or floured!

Chapter 6

Surprise *Mondaag*

As Rachel walked to school on Monday morning, her stomach quivered like it was filled with a team of fluttering butterflies flying in different directions. She carried a hunk of Jacob's birthday cake in her lunchbox. She planned to give it to Orlie during lunch today and hoped he would be surprised. She also hoped the gift might make him quit pestering her.

Jacob nudged Rachel's arm. "How come you're dawdling this morning? You're slower than a turtle walking uphill."

"Am not."

"Are so."

"I am not walking like a turtle, Jacob."

Jacob grunted. "Jah, you are. Your name ought to be Rachel Yoder, the Slowpoke Turtle, and if you don't walk faster, we'll be late for school." He poked her arm again. "Why do you always drag your feet every Mondaag morning?"

"I don't always walk slow on Monday mornings." Rachel kicked a small stone with the toe of her sneaker. "If you're worried about being late, go on ahead. Don't let me hold you back."

Jacob stopped walking and turned to face her. "You know I can't do that. Mom would be madder than a hornet trapped in a jar of honey if I let you walk to school alone."

Rachel knew Jacob was right. When Jacob graduated from school after eighth grade, then what would Mom do? Maybe by then she would think Rachel was old enough to go to school without a babysitter. Maybe by then she would realize that Rachel was growing up and could walk alone.

As a bright yellow school bus rumbled past, Jacob grabbed Rachel's hand and pulled her farther to the shoulder of the road. Rachel looked at the English children staring out their windows. She wondered if she were English and attended one of their public schools, if she'd have to put up with anyone mean like Orlie Troyer. She supposed there were boys like Orlie in every school, but that didn't make it any easier to think about facing him again this morning.

Jacob nudged Rachel again.

"What?"

"That hurry-up cake you made for my birthday on Saturday tasted pretty good, even if Mom did have to dig it out of the pan."

Rachel wasn't sure if that was supposed to be a compliment or if Jacob was teasing her again, but she decided not to make an issue of it. "Danki," she muttered, quickening her pace.

"Now you're walking too fast," Jacob complained. "Can't you find a happy medium?"

Rachel just kept on walking. Her brother was obviously looking for an argument this morning.

By the time Rachel and Jacob entered the schoolhouse, the butterflies in Rachel's stomach quieted. However, at noontime, Rachel's butterflies returned when her teacher announced that it was time for the scholars to eat their lunches. Should she give Orlie the piece of cake or forget about the idea? What if he didn't like hurry-up cake with strawberry icing? What if her gift didn't make him stop picking on her?

She drew in a deep breath and hurried over to the shelf where the lunchboxes were kept.

Orlie was already outside, sitting in his usual spot on the front porch. He looked at Rachel and wiggled his eyebrows. "Got any tuna sandwiches in your lunchbox today?" he asked with a silly grin.

Rachel shook her head. "I packed my own lunch this morning. I made a peanut butter and jelly sandwich."

He smacked his lips. "Peanut butter's pretty tasty, but I like tuna better."

Rachel wrinkled her nose in disgust. "I—uh— brought you something for dessert," she said, sitting beside him.

Orlie leaned toward Rachel. His breath tickled her neck, and she smelled the pungent aroma of garlic. She held her breath as she reached into her lunchbox for the cake and handed it to him.

His eyebrows lifted. "What's this?"

"It's some of my brother's birthday cake, and I baked it myself."

As Orlie pulled the lid off the container, his eyebrows rose higher. "This cake sure looks strange. How come it's shaped so funny?"

"It stuck to the pan and we had to dig it out." Rachel paused and licked her lips. "But it tastes okay, so it's safe to eat."

"My mamm bakes lots of cakes, and none of 'em has ever looked like this." Orlie puckered his lips and made an *oink-oink-oink* sound. "This looks like something that should have been fed to the hogs. Maybe you should take some baking lessons from my mamm."

Rachel clamped her lips together. *That's what I get for trying to be nice.* Giving Orlie a gift hadn't stopped him from saying unkind things to her. In fact, it seemed to have made things worse. She shouldn't have bothered bringing Orlie a gift. He sure didn't deserve one—especially when he'd acted so ungrateful and had said mean things about her baking skills.

Orlie continued to stare at the cake as he wrinkled his nose, like it smelled bad. Maybe it was his own dreadful breath he was smelling.

Feeling like a balloon that had been popped with a pin, Rachel said, "If you don't want it, then just throw it away."

"If you don't want it, then just throw it away," he repeated.

Rachel was about to say something more, when Jacob and two other boys, Nate and Samuel, walked by. Nate stopped in front of them. "How come you're sittin' with her?" he asked, pointing at Rachel.

Orlie shrugged and his ears turned bright red.

"Maybe she's his *aldi*." Samuel snickered. "Orlie likes Rachel," he said in a singsong voice. "Orlie likes Rachel, and she's his aldi."

"No, I'm not Orlie's girlfriend!" Rachel scooted quickly away from Orlie and reached into her lunchbox to retrieve the peanut butter and jelly sandwich she'd made. She took one bite, then dropped it back into the lunchbox. Her appetite was gone.

After lunch, Rachel's teacher clapped her hands and asked for the class's attention. "Judging from the way many of you chose several books to read the last time the bookmobile visited our school, I thought it would be fun to have each of you in grades three to six write a story."

Rachel's cousin raised her hand.

"Yes, Mary?"

"What kind of story?"

Elizabeth tapped her pencil against her chin. "Well, let's see now. . .I think it should be a made-up story, but you can base it on a real person or some kind of true happening."

Orlie's hand shot up.

"What is it, Orlie?"

"Should it be about someone living or dead?"

"Either," the teacher replied. "Just make sure you change things enough so the story is fiction and not something that actually happened."

"Oh, okay."

Elizabeth tapped her pencil on her desk. "You can spend the next hour writing the story, and then we'll do something else that should be both fun and interesting."

Rachel wasn't excited about writing a story. She wished she could draw a picture instead, but she knew better than to disobey the teacher, so she set right to work on her story about the most unusual person she'd ever met.

Sometime later, Elizabeth clapped her hands together again and said, "Time's up. Now you will each read what you've written. Rachel, would you like to go first?"

Rachel knew her teacher's question wasn't really a question. It was a direct command for Rachel to get out of her seat, walk to the front of the class, and read the story she'd written. She took a deep breath and swallowed hard, hoping she wouldn't throw up. If she'd known she would be expected to read her story in front of everyone, she would have written something else.

Slowly, Rachel stood. Her legs felt like bags of rocks had been tied to them, as she walked to the front of the room, carrying her notebook in her shaking hands.

Elizabeth smiled. "Go ahead, Rachel."

Rachel fought the temptation to bite off a fingernail and licked her lips instead. "Once there was a horse named Otis." She paused and cleared her throat. "Otis was an unusual horse because he smelled like a stinking rose and liked to eat weird things. Most horses eat hay, oats, and corn, but not Otis—he liked to eat tuna sandwiches and garlic cloves."

As Rachel continued with her story, her cheeks became hotter. Did Orlie realize her story was about him? Did the teacher and the whole class know that, too? Rachel finished the story by saying, "So, if you ever meet a horse that smells like a stinking rose and likes to eat weird food, you'll know it was Otis."

Rachel rushed back to her seat. She wished she could dash for the door and run all the way home. She didn't know what had possessed her to write such a story. Had it been her way of getting even with Orlie for saying mean things about her cake?

She grimaced. *I thought I was done with trying to get even. I thought I had decided to try and be nice to Orlie.* She reflected on the verse from Luke 6:31: "Do to others as you would have them do to you." *I wouldn't want someone to write a story about me and say bad things—not even a made-up story.*

"That was an interesting story, Rachel." Elizabeth's forehead wrinkled. Then she nodded at Orlie. "Now it's your turn, Orlie."

As Orlie passed Rachel's desk, he gave her a sidelong glance. She noticed how red his ears were, and she wondered if it was because of her story or if he felt nervous about reading his own story in front of the class.

Orlie shifted from one foot to the other, and his hands shook as he held on to his piece of paper.

"Go ahead, Orlie, we're waiting," Elizabeth prompted.

He cleared his throat and began. "Rosie the Raccoon had a problem." He paused and cleared his throat two more times. "Rosie's problem was that she didn't know how to bake. In fact, she baked a cake once that stuck to the pan and looked like pig food."

Rachel's ears burned, and she gripped the sides of her desk so hard her knuckles turned white. *Orlie wrote that story about me! Rosie the Raccoon didn't bake a cake that stuck to the pan. I did!* She glanced around the room. *I wonder if everyone knows.*

"Not being able to bake wasn't Rosie's only problem," Orlie said. "She was a picky eater who threw away her tuna fish sandwich when she thought no one was looking."

He continued with his story, telling how Rosie got dizzy one day when she was twirling on a tree branch. Then she got sick and threw up.

Rachel clenched her teeth. *He'll be sorry. Orlie doesn't deserve for me to be nice to him.*

On the way home from school, Rachel felt so sorry for herself that she wasn't watching her steps and tripped on a rock. *Plop!* She fell and skinned both knees. "Ouch! That really hurts," she whimpered.

Instead of offering sympathy, Jacob scolded her for not paying attention to where she was going and accused her of daydreaming.

"I was not daydreaming," she argued.

Jacob snickered. "You were probably thinking about that story Orlie read." He pointed at

Rachel. "It was about you, wasn't it? What was your name? Rosie the Raccoon?"

She grunted but didn't say anything. Nothing Rachel could say would make her feel better anyway. She just wanted to get home, clean her knees, and take a nap. That is, if Mom didn't have too many chores waiting for her to do.

When they arrived home a short time later, Jacob headed straight for the barn, and Rachel trudged wearily toward the house. She had just stepped onto the porch, when she noticed two of Mom's potted plants had been tipped over. Dirt was everywhere, and the plant stems were broken. She suspected her kitten had caused the mess, because Cuddles lay on the porch next to one of the pots, licking her dirty paws. Mom stood nearby, tapping her foot and clicking her tongue.

"Bad kitten!" Rachel scolded, shaking her finger in front of Cuddles's nose. "My whole Mondaag's gone bad, and now I come home to this?"

"What happened that made your Monday go bad?" Mom asked, looking concerned.

"More trouble with Orlie during school, and then I fell on the way home and skinned my knees." Rachel motioned to the overturned pot. "I'll change out of my school clothes and clean up this mess as soon as I've put some bandages on my knees."

"Would you like me to take a look at your knees?" Mom asked with a worried frown.

Rachel shook her head. "They're not so bad. I'll be all right." Rachel hurried up the stairs before her mother could ask any more questions. She figured if Mom knew the details of her horrible day, she would give her a lecture, and Rachel might even be given more chores to do.

By the time Rachel had bandaged her sore knees, changed out of her school clothes, and cleaned up the mess Cuddles had made on the porch, she was exhausted. Mom said Rachel could play until it was time to start supper, but Rachel was too tired to play. She decided to sit on the porch and blow bubbles with the metal wand Pap had given her for her birthday.

"At least nobody gave me a crumbly old cake that stuck to the pan and looked like it should have been fed to the *sei*," Rachel grumbled, as she stared at the pan of soapy water sitting beside her on the porch.

"What was that about hogs?"

Rachel looked up and saw an elderly Amish man walking across the grass, carrying a black suitcase. He wore dark trousers held up by suspenders, a light blue shirt, and a straw hat. He walked with a slight limp, and his hair and beard were mostly gray.

He lifted his hand and waved. "*Wie geht's*— how are you?"

Rachel squinted against the glare of the sun as she stared at him.

The man stepped onto the porch and grinned at her. "Don't you know who I am, Rachel?"

"Grandpa Schrock?"

He nodded and sat beside her on the step. "Surprised to see me, are you?"

"Oh, jah. We didn't expect you'd be making the trip from Ohio until it was almost time for Esther's wedding."

"Thought I'd come to Pennsylvania a little sooner and surprise you." Grandpa patted Rachel's arm. "That will give me more time to spend with you and the family."

Rachel nodded. Grandpa Schrock's last visit had been a lot of fun. Rachel had been two years younger then, but she could still remember Grandpa sitting on the porch swing, sharing his bag of peanuts as he told her stories. Since he'd arrived almost a month before Esther's wedding, she figured they would have lots of time to do fun things together.

Mom stepped onto the porch with a curious look on her face. "I thought I heard voices, but I figured your daed and Henry were still in the fields, so—"

Grandpa turned toward her, and Mom's face broke into a huge smile. "Oh, Papa, what a surprise! Where did you come from?"

"Ohio. Where do you think?" he asked with a deep chuckle.

"Ach, you're such a tease." Mom and Grandpa hugged each other. Then Mom reached under her glasses to wipe away her tears. "We didn't expect you until the end of October, since Esther isn't getting married until the first Thursday of November."

"I decided to come early and surprise you. When my bus pulled into the station in Lancaster, I spotted one of your English neighbors and asked him to give me a ride over here." He hugged her again. "Are you glad to see me, daughter?"

Mom nodded. "Oh, jah, I'm always glad to see my daed."

Seeing the joy on her mother's face and knowing Grandpa would be with them for a whole month made Rachel smile, too. Maybe today wasn't such a bad Mondaag after all.

Chapter 7

More Surprises

"For a little girl whose sister is getting married in a few days, you sure look sad," Grandpa said as he sat beside Rachel at the breakfast table one morning in late October. "Are you going to miss your big sister when she moves out of the house?"

Rachel glanced at Esther, who sat across from her. "I will miss my sister, but I'll miss you, too, Grandpa." For several days, Rachel had been thinking about the day Grandpa would return to Ohio, and how she wished he didn't have to go.

Grandpa's bushy, gray eyebrows lifted as he glanced at Pap and Mom. "Didn't either of you tell her my surprise?"

Mom shook her head. "We figured we should let you do the telling."

"Tell me what, Grandpa?" Rachel asked, leaning closer to him. "What surprise do you have?"

"I won't return to Ohio after Esther and Rudy's wedding."

Rachel's mouth dropped open. "You won't?"

"Nope. Your folks have invited me to live here. If you have no objections, I'll stay here for good."

Rachel thought this was such a wonderful surprise that she could hardly stay in her seat! Over the last few weeks, she and Grandpa had only spent a little time together. Now, with him staying permanently, they would have plenty of time together. They could do so many fun things—blow bubbles with Rachel's new wand, drive to the pond in one of Pap's buggies, take long walks to the stream, and tease Cuddles with string. Even having to put up with Orlie wouldn't seem as bad, because every day after school Grandpa would be waiting for Rachel at home.

Rachel reached over and took Grandpa's hand. "I'm real glad you're staying."

He grinned and squeezed her fingers. "Jah, me, too."

When Rachel arrived at school that morning, she received yet another surprise. A plump, red apple sat in the middle of her desk. She picked it up and turned to Mary. "Did you bring me this?"

Mary shook her head. "It was there when I came into the room."

Rachel opened the lid on her desk and placed the apple inside. She figured she would eat it at lunchtime.

Sometime later, Teacher Elizabeth announced that it was time for lunch, and Rachel hurried to get her lunchbox. Since it was raining outside, everyone sat at their desks to eat their lunches.

As the rain beat against the schoolhouse windows, Rachel ate her peanut butter and jelly sandwich, followed by two chunky chocolate chip cookies. She washed them down with her thermos of milk. She was about to put her lunchbox away, when she remembered the plump red apple.

Rachel pulled the apple out of her desk and savored the first bite. *Umm. . .this is so sweet and juicy.*

"How's that apple taste?" Orlie asked, tapping Rachel on the shoulder.

She turned around. "It's good."

He grinned at her and blinked a couple of times. "I picked it from one of our apple trees this morning."

Rachel's mouth dropped open. A stream of apple juice dribbled down her chin. "You—you put the apple on my desk?"

"That's right. I put it on your desk early this morning, before you got to school."

"Why?"

"I wanted to surprise you."

Rachel was surprised, all right. Especially since Orlie hadn't said a word to her for several weeks. She hadn't spoken to him either. In fact, ever since the day Rachel and Orlie had written those fiction stories about each other, neither had said more than a few words to one another. It was better that way, Rachel decided—better for her, at least.

Rachel stared at the tasty apple. She'd never expected to get anything from Orlie—at least nothing nice. Maybe he was tired of making her life miserable and had decided to make amends. Maybe he wasn't such a bad fellow after all.

"Danki," she murmured.

"You're welcome." Orlie leaned forward a bit, and Rachel leaned backward—in case his mother had given him some garlic to eat again this morning. "I hear that your sister's gettin' married soon," he said.

"That's right. This Thursday."

He grinned. "Guess I'll see you there, 'cause my family and I have been invited to the wedding."

A sense of dread crept up Rachel's spine. Then she looked at the apple in her hand and decided having Orlie at the wedding might not be so bad. At least he was being nice now. It wasn't like she'd have to hang around him all day. *Crunch.* She took another bite of the apple. It sure was tasty.

Rachel bit into it again, only this time she felt something rubbery and slimy touch her lips. She wrinkled her nose and spit the piece of apple into her hand. "That is so ekelhaft!"

"What's so disgusting?"

"This!" Rachel's hand shook as she held it out so Orlie could see what she had almost eaten.

Orlie's eyebrows arched upwards. "Ach, there was a little critter in that apple."

Rachel gritted her teeth. "You gave me a wormy apple on purpose, didn't you?"

He shook his head. "How could I know a worm was inside?"

Rachel turned the apple over and studied it closely. Sure enough, she saw a small wormhole near the stem. How could she have been so stupid? She should have looked the apple over thoroughly before taking a bite. She should have known Orlie wouldn't have given her anything nice. He'd probably given her the wormy apple just to be mean.

She plunked the apple on Orlie's desk. "You are *uninvited* to Esther's wedding!"

He looked stunned. "Why?"

"Anyone who would give someone a wormy apple shouldn't be allowed to attend anyone's wedding."

"But, but. . .I—I didn't know. . . ."

"Humph! And I suppose you didn't know who you were writing about when you wrote that goofy story about Rosie the Raccoon?"

Orlie shrugged. "Knew it about as well as you knew who Otis the Horse was supposed to be."

Rachel whirled around and closed her lunchbox with a *snap*. Learning that Grandpa would be staying in Pennsylvania had been a good morning surprise. But receiving a wormy apple and hearing that Orlie planned to attend Esther's wedding were two afternoon surprises she could have done without!

As Rachel climbed out of bed on Thursday morning, excitement filled her soul. She'd spent several days helping Mom and Esther clean the house for Esther's wedding. Yesterday, many of their Amish friends had come to help, too. It had been a lot of work, but the house was now spotless, and everything was ready for the wedding.

Rachel skipped across the room in her bare feet, smiling. She wouldn't have to go to school today. All of the children who'd been invited to the wedding would also be excused. Not Orlie, though. He'd be sitting at his desk with plenty of work to do, because Rachel had uninvited him to her sister's wedding after he'd given her that wormy apple.

"It serves him right for being so mean," she muttered as she pulled her bottom dresser drawer open. Orlie needed to be taught a lesson, and Rachel hoped by missing Esther's wedding, he might learn that he couldn't go around teasing all the time without suffering the consequences of his actions.

Rachel picked up the small package wrapped in white tissue paper that she'd placed in her drawer. Then she tiptoed across the hall to Esther's bedroom.

"Come in," Esther called, when Rachel knocked on the door.

Rachel stepped into the room and spotted Esther standing by her window. "*Guder mariye*, bride-to-be."

Esther turned to face Rachel. "Good morning. What do you have in your hands?"

"It's a wedding present for you," Rachel said, handing the package to her sister. "I made it myself."

Esther placed the gift on the bed, removed the wrapping, and lifted out a white hankie with a lacy edge. In one corner, Rachel had embroidered the letters E.K.—which would be Esther's initials after she married Rudy King.

"What a nice surprise," Esther said, hugging Rachel. "Danki so much."

"You're welcome." Rachel was pleased that her sister liked the gift. It had been a labor of love, since Rachel didn't like to sew much.

Esther motioned toward her door. "I guess we'd better go help Mom with breakfast now. Today's my big day, and I wouldn't want to be late for my own wedding."

Rachel giggled and followed her sister.

Downstairs, Mom scurried around the kitchen with a spatula in her hand. She halted and gave Esther a kiss on the cheek. "How's the bride feeling on this fine fall morning?"

Esther smiled, her cheeks turning pink as a rose. "I'm a bit *naerfich*, so you'd better give me something to do that will help settle my nerves."

Mom nudged Esther toward the table. "While I cook some oatmeal, you can help Rachel set the table."

"Okay, Mom." Esther's hands shook as she pulled paper napkins out of the basket in the center of the table.

"Why are you so nervous, sister?" Rachel asked. "You're shaking like a maple tree on a windy day."

"I'm nervous about marrying Rudy today."

"Then don't get married. Stay here with us."

"I love Rudy and want to marry him." Esther smiled. "Guess I'm really more excited than nervous."

"Every bride has a right to be nervous on her wedding day," Mom put in.

Rachel watched Esther place the napkins around the table, where each family member would sit. "I still don't see why Esther wants to get married," she said as she set spoons and knives on top of each napkin. "I'm never getting married. . .not ever!"

Mom chuckled. "You'll change your mind someday. Just wait and see."

At eight thirty sharp, more than one hundred guests filled the house to witness the marriage of Esther Yoder and Rudy King. Men and women sat on backless wooden benches in separate sections of the room, just as they did during their regular church services. After everyone was seated, Rudy's brother-in-law, Michael, announced the first song from the hymnbook called the *Ausbund*. On the third line of the song, the ministers stood and left the room. Rachel knew they were going upstairs to a room that had been prepared for them on the second floor. Rudy and Esther followed so they could receive counsel and words of encouragement before the ceremony. While they sang the second song, Rachel saw Orlie Troyer sitting across the room with some other boys.

She clenched her fingers into tight little balls in her lap. *What's he doing here? I told Orlie he was uninvited to Esther's wedding.*

Rachel spotted Orlie's mother sitting on the women's side, with Orlie's little sisters, Becky and Malinda. On the men's side, Orlie's father sat with Orlie's older brothers, Isaac, Jonas, and James, who were in their teens and had already finished school.

She sighed. *I guess if Orlie's family came today, they would expect him to be here, too. He probably never even told his folks I said he couldn't come. Sure hope he doesn't do anything to ruin my sister's wedding.*

Rachel's attention was drawn to the front of the room again when Esther and Rudy returned to their seats. The ministers entered a short time later, and Herman Lapp, one of the ministers, delivered the first sermon. Then came a time of silent prayer before the longer sermon, given by Bishop Wagler.

Rachel fidgeted on her bench. She wondered how much longer the ceremony would last. She thought about what she would say to Orlie after the wedding service.

When the bishop finally finished his sermon, he cleared his throat and said, "We have two people who have agreed to enter the state of matrimony, Rudy King and Esther Yoder." He paused and looked at the congregation. "If any here has objection, he now has the opportunity to make it known."

The room was so quiet Rachel thought she could have heard a feather fall to the floor. Surely no one would try and stop Esther and Rudy from getting married.

Bishop Wagler had just opened his mouth to speak again, when a streak of gray and white darted across the room.

Rachel gasped. "Oh, no. . .it's Cuddles, and she's after a maus!"

The cat zipped this way and that, swatting her paw every time she came near the mouse. The mouse zoomed under a bench on the men's side of the room. Grandpa reached down, trying to catch it in his hands. *Zip! Zip!* The mouse darted away, escaping not only Grandpa, but every other man who tried to capture it. Walter Troyer, Orlie's father, tried to stomp the poor mouse with his boot, but the tiny critter escaped to the women's side of the room.

"Ach, get away from me!" Anna Miller shouted, as the mouse ran across her shoes. Anna and the ladies near her screamed and jumped onto their bench.

Cuddles leaped into the air and landed in Sarah King's lap. The elderly woman, who was Rudy's grandmother, turned white as snow and nearly fainted. Rachel's mother reached over to steady the poor woman.

"Everyone, please calm down!" Bishop Wagler shouted over the high-pitched screams. "Please take your seats and let the wedding continue."

Rachel knew the wedding couldn't continue until either the cat or the mouse had been caught. She did the only thing she could think to do—she jumped off her bench and chased after Cuddles. Round the room they went—the mouse going one way, the cat following, and Rachel right on its tail. Several men shouted directions.

Suddenly Orlie joined the chase. He dove for the mouse but missed. The critter darted right up Deacon Byler's leg.

Rachel gasped and grabbed her kitten as it scooted past. At least one problem was solved. She was about to haul Cuddles out the door when the mouse skittered up the deacon's chest, pitter-patted across his shoulders, and darted down his other pant leg.

The deacon grunted, and Orlie made another

dive for the mouse. This time he grabbed it by the tail. The men nodded. The women sighed. Rachel just stood there, shaking her head. She figured Orlie had only tried to capture the mouse so he would look good in everyone's eyes.

He probably brought the mouse into the house in the first place, Rachel thought. *He probably just wanted to play another trick on me.*

As Rachel went out the door with Cuddles in her arms, she mumbled, "I wish Orlie Troyer would move back to Indiana."

Chapter 8

Misadventures

Rachel kicked a small stone with the toe of her sneaker as she headed to the chicken coop. She felt fretful, but not because of her chores. She dreaded going to school the day after Esther's wedding and facing Orlie again.

Rachel had been scolded by both Mom and Pap because her cat had disrupted the wedding. After Cuddles and the mouse had been put outside, the rest of the ceremony had been fine. Rachel had tried to explain that the cat had probably entered with guests who came into the house, but Pap had been quick to remind her that Cuddles should have been locked in the basement during the wedding.

As far as Rachel was concerned, the whole episode had been Orlie's fault. She was sure he'd brought the mouse into the house in order to cause an uproar.

Rachel entered the chicken coop and held her nose. She didn't want to be in this smelly building any longer than she had to. She opened the bag of grain, scooped some out with a dipper, and filled each feeding tray. Next it was time to give the chickens water.

Rachel picked up a watering dish and stepped out of the coop. Then she rinsed out the container, filled it with fresh water, and hurried back across the yard.

Squawk! Squawk! Rachel had just stepped back into the coop, when a chicken flapped its wings and flew up in her face. As Rachel tried to shoo the chicken away, the dish flipped out of her hand, and water went everywhere. "Oh, no. Now I have to start all over," she moaned.

Rachel had only taken a few steps toward the door, when her foot slipped on the slimy, wet floor. "*Umph!*" She landed hard. Clucking chickens flew everywhere, bumping into Rachel, pecking at each other, and sending feathers flying in every direction.

"Always trouble somewhere," Rachel grumbled.

She scrambled to her feet and stared at her rumpled, wet dress. Now she would have to change clothes before school.

Rachel went back outside to fill the watering dish, only this time she carefully screwed on the lid.

When Rachel was heading back to the house, she heard a horse whinny. Maybe she had enough time to say hello to old Tom.

Rachel scampered to the fence separating their yard from the pasture. "Come on, Tom. Come and get your nose rubbed."

Nee–eee. Tom pawed at the ground.

Rachel climbed onto the fence and leaned over, extending her hand. "Come over to me, boy. I can't reach you from here."

Nee–ee! Nee–ee! The horse continued to paw at the ground.

"What's the matter with you, Tom?" Rachel waited to see what Tom would do, but he wouldn't budge.

Grunting, Rachel lifted one leg and eased herself over the fence. Once her feet touched the ground, she moved over to stand beside the horse. "Easy, boy. Easy, now," she said, reaching out to touch Tom.

He bent his head and nuzzled her hand.

"Sorry, but I don't have a treat for you this morning. Guess I should have brought a sugar cube or an apple for you, huh?"

Tom whinnied and bounced his head up and down, as though agreeing with her.

A field mouse scampered through the grass at Rachel's feet, reminding her of the mouse at Esther's wedding. Her fingers curled into her palms until they dug into her flesh. *Orlie should be punished for doing that, and for giving me that wormy apple the other day, too.*

"Guess I'd better get back to the house now," Rachel said, giving Tom another pat. "I'll come visit you again soon."

Suddenly, the mean old goose that sometimes chased Rachel waddled up to Tom, squawking and pecking at the horse's legs. Tom flicked his ears, sidestepped, and kicked his back leg out at the goose. The goose flapped her wings and screeched. When Tom's foot came down, it landed right on the toe of Rachel's sneaker. She squealed and jumped out of Tom's way. So much for doing her good deed for the day.

"Every time I try to do something nice, things go bad," she muttered, as she limped away.

By the time Rachel got back to the house, her

foot hurt so bad she could barely stand.

"What's wrong, Rachel?" Mom asked when Rachel hopped into the kitchen. "Did you hurt yourself in the chicken coop?"

Rachel shook her head as tears filled her eyes. She had been able to keep from crying until she saw the look of sympathy on Mom's face. Now she wanted to dissolve into a puddle of tears. "I—I went out to the pasture to see Tom, then the crazy old goose came along and—"

"Did that cantankerous critter attack you like she did this summer? Because if she did, I'll have your daed put her down."

"The goose didn't attack me. She was after old Tom." Rachel hobbled to a chair at the table. "Tom kicked out at her, and his foot landed on my toe." She sniffed. "It hurts something awful."

Mom knelt in front of Rachel and removed the sneaker and black stocking on Rachel's right foot.

Rachel gasped when she saw how terrible her big toe looked. Not only was it swollen, but it was purple. "No wonder it hurts so bad," she whimpered. "Do—do you think it's broken?"

Mom's glasses had slipped to the middle of her nose. She pushed them back in place as she studied Rachel's toe. "It could be, but we can't do much for a broken toe. We'll need to put ice on it. And you'll need to stay off that foot for a few days."

Rachel's mood brightened. "Does that mean I don't have to go to school today?"

Mom nodded. "Since this is Friday, you'll have the weekend to rest your toe. You should feel up to going to school by Monday."

Rachel didn't like the pain shooting from her toe all the way up her leg. But if it meant missing school today, she was glad it had happened. She'd avoid seeing Orlie. She could also lie on the sofa all day with her foot propped on pillows and read her favorite book.

Mom rose to her feet. "Your daed's still doing chores with Grandpa and the boys. I'll have him carry you upstairs to your room as soon as he comes in."

"Can't I lie on the sofa in the living room?"

Mom's forehead wrinkled. "Oh, I don't know, Rachel. Jacob will be at school, but everyone else will be busy all day getting rid of the mess from yesterday. And we still have to clean the living room."

"I won't be in the way, I promise."

Mom shook her head. "I think it would be best if you stay in your room."

Rachel didn't argue. She was so glad to stay

home from school that it really didn't matter where she spent the day.

Rachel reclined on her bed with her foot propped on two thick pillows and an ice bag resting on her toe. She thought about all the fun things she wished she could be doing. Even helping Mom, Pap, Grandpa, Esther, and Rudy clean the house would be better than lying alone with nothing to do but stare at the ceiling. She couldn't even play with Cuddles, because after what had happened yesterday, Mom had banned Rachel's cat from the house until further notice.

Rachel glanced at the clock on the table by her bed. She wondered what her classmates were doing right now. *Probably spelling,* she thought with regret. Spelling was Rachel's favorite subject. She always did well whenever she had a spelling test.

"How are things going?" Mom asked, poking her head into Rachel's room.

Rachel shrugged. "I'm bored. I don't have anything to do. I wish I could be downstairs with everyone else."

"Maybe later, after we finish cleaning." Mom lifted the ice bag from Rachel's toe and squinted. "Looks like the swelling's going down, but you

need to stay off that foot for the rest of the day."
She turned toward the door. "I'll refill your ice bag."

"Danki."

Several minutes later, Mom returned. Besides
the ice bag, she held the small sewing kit she'd
given Rachel for her birthday. "Since you're bored,
I thought you could do some mending for me."

Mom placed the sewing kit on the table by
Rachel's bed and handed her one of Pap's socks
with a hole in it.

Rachel frowned as she laid the sock beside her
on the bed. "Oh, Mom. . .do I have to?"

Mom nodded and headed across the room,
calling over her shoulder, "Pap will carry you down
when it's time for lunch."

The door clicked shut, and Rachel sighed.
She didn't care much for sewing, because she still
couldn't sew a straight seam. Well, maybe it didn't
matter how well she sewed, since no one would see
the mended hole in Pap's sock.

Rachel reached for her sewing kit, threaded
the needle, tied a knot, and picked up the sock. In
and out, in and out, the needle went, until the hole
finally disappeared. Her stitching was uneven and
thicker in some parts than others, but at least she'd
finished the job. Now she only needed to cut the

thread and tie a knot. She picked up the scissors and held the sock up where she could see the tiny thread. *Snip.* "Rats! I missed." She tried once more. *Snip.* She missed again.

"What's wrong with me?" Rachel wailed. "Can't I do anything right today?" She leaned closer and lifted the scissors for the third time. *Snip.* The thread still clung to the needle, but a piece of white ribbon lay in her lap.

Rachel reached up and touched the ties on her kapp. One tie was shorter than the other. "Oh, no! Now what have I done? I never should have gone to visit old Tom this morning." She flopped onto her pillow and thought about her horrible day. If only she'd returned to the house after feeding and watering the chickens, she wouldn't have gotten her toe stepped on. She would be in school right now, not sitting here looking at the tie she had cut by mistake. Even putting up with Orlie's teasing might have been better than sewing alone in her room. This was not a good day!

Chapter 9

Woolly Worm

"How's your toe feel today?" Grandpa asked as he took a seat on the porch beside Rachel on Sunday afternoon. Today was an off Sunday from church, so Rachel's parents had gone with Jacob and Henry to call on Grandpa and Grandma Yoder. Grandpa Schrock didn't want to go, and Rachel had decided to stay home with him.

"It's a little better now," Rachel said, removing her slipper and lifting her foot.

Grandpa leaned forward and squinted. "Hmm . . .still looks kind of purple, but the swelling's gone down. Think you'll be ready to go to school tomorrow?"

She shrugged. "My foot will be ready, but I'm not sure I will."

"Why?"

"I'm not looking forward to seeing Orlie again."

"He's that boy in your class who teases you, right?"

Rachel nodded.

Grandpa pursed his lips. "It seems you might do best to ignore the fellow."

"I've tried that and it doesn't work. Orlie keeps doing things to annoy me."

"Have you prayed about it, Rachel?" Grandpa asked, placing his hand on her shoulder.

She shook her head slowly, ashamed to admit that she hadn't prayed. She'd been so angry with Orlie she hadn't thought to pray about the matter.

Grandpa gently squeezed her shoulder. "When I was a boy my mamm always told me that prayer was the key to each new day and the lock for every night. There isn't much of anything that shouldn't be given to God in prayer."

"I guess you're right," Rachel said. "I'll try to remember to pray about Orlie."

Grandpa smiled. "Good girl." He meandered across the porch and plucked something off the wooden rail. "Well, well. . .what do you know?"

"What is it, Grandpa?"

"It's a woolly worm," he said, extending his hand out to her. "I used to see a lot of these in Holmes County, Ohio."

Rachel shrugged. "What's so special about a woolly worm? It's just an orange and black fuzzy caterpillar."

"Oh, no, Rachel. . .there's more to woolly worms than their color." Grandpa sat in the wicker chair again and closed his hand, trapping the woolly worm inside.

"Like what?" she asked.

"I was thinking about the woolly races."

Rachel tipped her head to one side. "Woolly races? What are those?"

"The woolly races involve a contest that's held in October during Charm Days." Grandpa uncurled his fingers and let the woolly worm creep around in his hand. "As many as eighty kinner take part in a contest to see whose woolly worm can be the first to make it to the top of a heavy piece of string." He chuckled, and Rachel noticed a twinkle in his blue eyes. "It's truly funny to see those youngsters clap, blow, whistle, and sing, trying to get their woolly worms up that string."

Feeling excitement zip up her spine, Rachel jumped out of the chair. "Got any ideas where I could find more woolly worms?"

"I might. Why?"

"I could take them to school and have a contest during recess."

Grandpa nodded and rose to his feet. "Sounds like a good idea to me." He faced Rachel, his expression becoming serious. "You'll have to abide by one important rule, though."

"What rule is that?"

"No touching the worm with your hands to make him move up the string."

Rachel nodded as her excitement grew. "I'll make sure everyone who takes part in the race knows that rule."

"I have something fun planned for recess this morning," Rachel said to Jacob as they headed for school on Monday morning.

"Oh, yeah? What?"

"I'm going to have a woolly worm race."

"A what?"

"A woolly worm race. Yesterday Grandpa told me about a contest that involves racing woolly worms. He helped me find a bunch of woolly caterpillars, and I've got eleven of them right here," Rachel said, lifting her lunchbox.

Jacob wrinkled his nose. "You put caterpillars in your lunchbox?"

She nodded.

"I hope you don't plan to eat them, Rachel."

"Of course not, silly. I'm going to have a woolly worm race during recess. The ten woolly worms the other kids will race are inside a cottage cheese carton in my lunchbox." She grinned. "I put Speedy in a yogurt cup by himself."

"Speedy?"

"That's right. Since Speedy's the fastest caterpillar we found, I've decided to race him."

Jacob rolled his eyes and shook his head. "What a bensel you are, little sister."

Rachel didn't bother to argue. She figured Jacob was probably jealous because he hadn't thought to have a woolly worm race at school. He'd see soon enough how much fun racing woolly worms could be.

When they entered the schoolyard, Rachel felt more and more excited. She and Grandpa had spent several hours searching for woolly worms. They'd looked under piles of leaves, in the compost heap behind Mom's vegetable garden, and behind a tree's bark. They'd even found a couple of worms by the side of the road. Rachel was sure the school children would enjoy the woolly worm race. Since she'd practiced the day before with Speedy, she was sure she would win.

At the school, Rachel opened her lunchbox. She placed the cottage cheese and yogurt containers on the floor under her desk. That way the woolly worms would have more air to breath through the tiny holes she'd poked in the lids. Teacher Elizabeth didn't seem to notice what Rachel was doing, as she was busy writing the math lesson on the blackboard.

"I brought something fun with me this morning," Rachel whispered, when Mary sat down across from her.

Mary leaned over as far as she could. "What is it?"

"You'll find out at recess."

Mary shrugged and turned to face the front of the class, where Elizabeth stood with a Bible in her hands. Rachel barely listened as their teacher read from God's Word. She could only think about Speedy and the race she was sure he would win for her. It was hard to concentrate on the lesson after the time of prayer and singing. At recess time, Rachel reached under her desk, grabbed both containers, and bounded from the room.

"May I have your attention, everyone?" she shouted as she stood in the middle of the schoolyard.

A few girls and Orlie came over to see what Rachel wanted. Most of the boys, including Jacob, ignored her and kept playing.

"What's up, Rachel?" Mary asked, scrunching her nose.

"Are you planning to eat lunch early today?" Orlie laughed and pointed to the cottage cheese and yogurt containers in her hands. "Do you want us to watch you eat it, huh?"

She scowled. "What I have inside these containers is much better than cottage cheese or yogurt."

"What do you have?" Aaron King asked. "Is it something to eat?"

Rachel shook her head. "It's woolly worms. I brought them so we can have a contest."

"What kind of contest?" Phoebe Wagler, the bishop's granddaughter, wanted to know.

"It's a race to see whose woolly worm will

reach the top of the string first."

Orlie's eyebrows furrowed. "What string? I don't see any string." He turned to face Mary. "Do you see any string?"

Mary shook her head, then looked at Rachel with questioning eyes. "What string are you talking about?"

"This." Rachel reached into her jacket pocket and pulled out a ball of heavy string. "We can cut it into long pieces. Then we'll tie one end to the top fence rail and the other end to the bottom rail. We'll each set our woolly worm on the string and see which one gets to the top first."

"But I don't have a woolly worm," Aaron said with a frown.

"Me neither," Mary put in.

Rachel lifted the cottage cheese carton. "They're right here. You can take your pick."

"What's inside the yogurt cup?" Orlie asked.

"That's Speedy. . .my woolly worm."

"Speedy, huh?" Orlie slowly shook his head. "I'll bet I can make any worm in that cottage cheese carton beat yours anytime."

"Bet you can't."

"Bet I can."

"Bet you can't."

"Bet I—"

Her cousin Mary stepped between them. "You're wasting time arguing. Just race the worms and see who wins."

"Good idea." Rachel marched across the schoolyard to the fence. With a few quick snips of the scissors she'd put in her pocket, she cut several pieces of string.

"Who wants to pick a worm?" she asked, opening the cottage cheese container.

Aaron jumped up and down. "I do! I do!"

"Me, too," Mary echoed.

"I'll take one," Phoebe said with a nod.

Soon, several other children had chosen a woolly worm to race.

"How about you, Orlie?" Rachel asked. "Aren't you going to pick one?"

He nodded. "Jah, sure. I was just waiting for everyone else to choose so you didn't think I'd gotten the best one, that's all."

Rachel opened the lid on the yogurt container. "As far as I'm concerned, Speedy's the best. He's fast! You'll see."

"Jah, well, I'll bet my worm can beat him." Orlie reached into the container and plucked out a fat woolly worm. "This critter's name is Tiger.

He's gonna beat every woolly worm here."

"We'll see about that." Rachel held up her hand. "Now, the rules are this: You can clap, sing, whistle, or blow on your worm to get him to move. But you can't touch him with your hands."

Everyone nodded in agreement.

"Okay, now, let's tie those strings to the fence and start the race!"

A few minutes later, ten children had lined up along the fence with woolly worms. Many of the scholars who had shown no interest in the contest now watched on the sidelines.

"Want me to signal when to start?" Jacob asked, stepping up to Rachel.

She shrugged. "Someone has to, so it may as well be you."

"All right then." Jacob cupped his hands around his mouth and breathed deeply. "One...two...three...go!"

Rachel put Speedy at the bottom of her string, tipped her head, and blew on his furry little body. "Go, Speedy. Get up that string, and be quick about it."

Mary clapped her hands and hollered, "*Dummle*, slowpoke. Hurry now, please."

Aaron King sang a silly song to try and get his worm to move. "Woolly, woolly, ding-dongding; woolly, woolly, you make me sing. Woolly, woolly, now do your thing; woolly, woolly, I'll soon be king."

Rachel's worm was halfway up the string when she heard several children shouting and clapping. "Go, Tiger, go! *Schnell*—quickly!"

She stopped blowing on Speedy to glance at Orlie and almost gagged. He had his mouth open and was nudging the woolly worm with his tongue.

Rachel wrinkled her nose. "That's so disgusting. Besides, you're cheating, Orlie."

"Am not," he said in a muffled voice. His tongue was still out. He sounded like a baby trying to talk. "You said no touching with your hands, not your tongue."

He glanced at her out of the corner of his eye.

Rachel wasn't sure if Orlie's worm was crawling so fast because Orlie was coaxing it with his tongue, or if the woolly worm moved along quickly in order to get away from Orlie's garlic breath. Rachel leaned over and blew so hard on Speedy that he nearly fell off the string. "I'm going to win this race, and I'll do it fair and square!" she shouted.

"That's what you think." Orlie wore a satisfied

smile as he prompted his worm with the end of his pointy tongue.

The children clapped and hollered—some cheered for Rachel, and others shouted for Orlie's woolly to win. Rachel was so busy blowing on Speedy and watching Tiger that she didn't even notice how the other children's worms were doing. Not until Aaron sang out, "My woolly won! My woolly won! We made it to the top. Jah, we're done!"

Rachel looked and her mouth dropped open. Sure enough, his woolly had reached the top of the string, two inches ahead of Rachel's, and at least one inch in front of Orlie's. "But—but I was sure my woolly would win," she mumbled.

"Oh, how sad." Orlie pretended to wipe tears from his eyes. Rachel gritted her teeth.

Everyone cheered, and Aaron bowed. "What's my prize for winning this woolly worm race?"

Everyone looked at Rachel. Her forehead wrinkled. She'd been so busy planning the race and thinking she would win that she hadn't even thought of a prize. "Well, I—"

"How about some chocolate chip cookies?" Elizabeth asked. She stepped up to Aaron and touched the top of his head.

His dark eyes widened, and he licked his lips. "You got some, Teacher?"

Elizabeth smiled. "Sure do. I brought chocolate chip cookies as a treat for the class today. Since your woolly won, I think I'll give you a few extra." She smiled at Rachel. "The woolly worm race was a good idea. How about if we do it again some other time?"

Rachel nodded. The race hadn't gone quite the way she'd wanted, but everyone seemed to enjoy it. Even though Speedy hadn't reached the top of the string first, at least Orlie and his pointy red tongue hadn't won.

Chapter 10

Substitute Teacher

When Rachel entered the schoolhouse one Friday morning, she was surprised to see Aaron King's aunt, Lovina, sitting at the teacher's desk. Lovina was a tall, thin woman who had never married. She still lived at home with her elderly parents. She had dark brown hair and almond-shaped eyes that were also brown. Rachel knew Lovina could be very stern. She wondered what Lovina was doing at the teacher's desk, and where Elizabeth was.

"Good morning, boys and girls," Lovina said, after everyone sat down. "I'll be your teacher for the next several weeks."

Rachel's mouth dropped open. No, this couldn't be. She didn't want a substitute teacher.

When Lovina opened her Bible for the

morning reading, Rachel raised her hand.

"What is it, Rachel?"

"Where's Elizabeth?"

"Her grandmother in Tennessee is ill. So Elizabeth has gone to help out." Lovina leaned slightly forward, with her elbows resting on the desk. "I'll be teaching your class until she gets back, sometime after Christmas."

Christmas? Rachel couldn't believe Elizabeth would be gone that long. What about the Christmas program? Would that be canceled if Elizabeth was still in Tennessee? Rachel felt badly that her teacher's grandmother was sick, but she wondered why Sharon Smucker, Elizabeth's helper, couldn't teach the class in her absence. However, she didn't ask the question. No point in saying something that might upset Lovina.

Rachel looked at Mary to get her reaction, but Mary gazed straight ahead.

Rachel sighed. She hoped Elizabeth's grandma got well real soon, so Elizabeth could return to Pennsylvania before Christmas.

Rachel felt a tap on her shoulder, and she turned around. "Little bensel, didn't you hear what the teacher said?" Orlie asked, wiggling his eyebrows.

"I—I guess not. What'd she say?"

"We're supposed to stand and recite the Lord's Prayer."

"Oh." Rachel pushed her chair back and stood. She had not only missed hearing the Bible reading, but she hadn't even heard Lovina announce that it was time to recite their morning prayer.

Rachel had a hard time concentrating on the prayer. It was even harder to keep her mind on the songs after that. It didn't help that Orlie stood beside her, blowing garlic breath in her face. Finally the scholars returned to their seats.

"This morning, before we begin our lessons," the teacher said with a nod, "I want to give everyone their parts for the Christmas play next month."

Rachel thought about the program the scholars always put on for their families shortly before Christmas. Last year, she had recited a poem. The year before that she'd sung a song with some other children. She wondered what her part in the program would be this year. She hoped she would be given something easy to say.

"Since Elizabeth won't be here, I'll be in charge of the program this year," the substitute teacher said. "We'll have some singing, recitations, and a few of you will act out the Nativity scene. The play I have written includes parts for Mary, Joseph, five shepherds, and two angels."

"What about the baby Jesus?" Lovina's nephew Aaron hollered without raising his hand. "Won't there be a part for Him, too?"

"We won't use a real baby," Lovina said, shaking her head. "And from now on, please raise your hand if you have a question."

Aaron's face turned cherry red and he slunk low in his seat. Rachel was glad she wasn't the one getting in trouble with the teacher or being embarrassed in front of the class. She'd had enough of that in the last few months.

Phoebe Byler lifted her hand.

Lovina nodded at Phoebe. "Yes?"

"How about using a faceless doll to play Baby Jesus' part?" Phoebe suggested. "I've got an old doll we can use."

"I have one, too!" Becky Esh shouted. She covered her mouth with her hand. "Oops. . .sorry for not raising my hand, Teacher."

Lovina nodded, and a smile tugged at the corners of her mouth. "We can talk about that later. Right now I want to assign your parts. Then, after lunch, we'll begin practicing for the program."

She walked to the blackboard, picked up a piece of chalk, and wrote the words "CHRISTMAS PROGRAM" in capital letters. "If you don't see your name on the blackboard, that means you'll either have a poem to recite or you'll be part of the group that will sing a few songs."

Rachel watched with interest as Lovina wrote "Angels" on the board. Under that, she listed: "Phoebe Byler, Mary Yoder." Next, Lovina wrote "Shepherds," followed by five names: "Jacob Yoder, Aaron King, Harvey Esh, Abner Clemmons, and Noah Stoltzfus."

Jacob will be happy to get the part of a shepherd, Rachel thought. She looked across the room and noticed that he was smiling. *He likes petting Grandpa Yoder's sheep. Maybe he'll be allowed to bring a sheep to the program so the play will seem more realistic.*

Rachel felt a nudge in her back, and she turned sharply. "Quit poking me, Orlie," she said through clenched teeth.

"Looks like we'll be workin' together," he said,

pointing to the blackboard.

Rachel looked at the chalkboard and nearly choked. The word "Mary" was written there, with Rachel's name underneath. But even worse was what was written beside that. It said: "Joseph," by the name "Orlie Troyer."

Rachel slunk farther down in her seat than Aaron had. Playing the part of Mary with Orlie as Joseph was the worst thing she could imagine. She had to figure a way out of it quickly. She raised her hand and waved it.

Lovina nodded at Rachel. "Yes?"

"Can't I do a recitation like I did last year? I'll even write my own poem if that would help."

Lovina shook her head. "I chose the parts based on who I thought would fit the roles best, and I picked you to play Mary."

"Oh, but my cousin's name is Mary, so shouldn't she be the one to play the part of baby Jesus' mother?"

Lovina took a seat behind her desk. "I've made my decision on who gets what parts. Now it's time to begin lessons, so please open your books."

Rachel went through the rest of the morning

feeling as if she had a bale of hay sitting on top of her head. She couldn't play the part of Mary in the Christmas program! Not with Orlie as Joseph! Orlie didn't like her; that was clear as glass. And she didn't care for him, either.

Rachel had seen other Christmas programs where the Nativity scene was acted out, so she knew what would be required of her in the role of Mary. She would have to sit on a stool behind a small wooden manager, and Joseph would be expected to stand right beside her. Just the thought of practicing every day with Orlie and sitting beside him during the program twisted Rachel's stomach in knots.

Maybe I could let old Tom step on my toe again, she thought as she returned to the schoolhouse after lunch recess. *Then my foot would be too sore to come to school.* She shook her head. That wouldn't work. When Mom heard that Rachel had been given the part of Mary, she would probably drive her to school in one of Pap's buggies every day, just so she could be there to practice, sore toe or not.

Rachel tapped her chin with the end of her pencil as she pondered the predicament she was in. If she prayed real hard, maybe Elizabeth's grandma would get well soon. Then Elizabeth could return to teaching school before the program. Surely Elizabeth would let Rachel out of being Mary. Or maybe Rachel could figure out some way to get exposed to the chicken pox or measles the week of the program. Then she'd be home sick in bed that day, not sitting beside Orlie in front of everyone she knew, feeling nervous about the possibility of forgetting her lines. What if Orlie decided to play a trick on her during the program? Why, the kids in class would make fun of her for weeks.

"All right now, scholars," Lovina announced. "I'm going to separate you into groups in order to practice for the Christmas program." She pointed to Mary and then to Phoebe. "You two angels can practice over there." She motioned to the left side of the room, and when Phoebe and Mary stood, Lovina handed them each a slip of paper. "Here are your lines, girls. They aren't hard, so you should be able to memorize them easily."

Next, she pointed to Jacob and the other shepherds. She instructed them to take their parts and practice at the back of the room.

Finally, Lovina nodded at Rachel and Orlie. "You two can practice your lines over there." She motioned to the corner of the room where the woodstove sat.

Rachel forced herself to walk to the teacher's desk. She took the slips of paper with hers and Orlie's parts and plodded across the room. She stared at the stove, wishing she could open the door and toss the paper into the burning flames. She figured that probably wouldn't do any good. The determined substitute would probably print another set of lines for Rachel and Orlie.

Orlie sauntered over to stand by Rachel, wearing a smug expression. "It'll be fun to have the best parts in the Christmas program, won't it?"

Fun for you maybe, because you can make my life miserable. Rachel plastered a smile on her face. For her, playing the part of Mary would be sheer torture.

As Rachel walked home from school that afternoon, she could only think about how awful it was to have a substitute teacher and how miserable she felt knowing Orlie would play Joseph. Throughout their practice time, Orlie had made wisecracks and messed up his lines just to confuse Rachel. While walking home, she usually enjoyed listening to the birds in the trees, looking for unusual shrubs, and watching the cars zip past. Not today.

"Why do you look so disagreeable?" Jacob asked, punching Rachel's arm. "You look like you've been sucking on sour grapes."

"I'm not happy about playing Mary in the Christmas program."

"Why?"

"Do you really have to ask?" Rachel groaned. "Orlie's playing Joseph, and you know Orlie and I don't get along."

"Maybe that's because you don't try hard enough to like him."

"I've tried every way I know to be nice to that ornery fellow. He always does something to get me riled," she answered.

"I'm sure that's why he does it." Jacob jabbed Rachel again. "I still think Orlie has a crush on you."

"He does not."

"Does so."

Rachel started to run. "Does not!" she called over her shoulder.

"Hey, wait! You know you're not supposed to walk home alone."

"I'm not walking; I'm running."

By the time Rachel reached home, she was panting, but she felt a little better about things.

Maybe it was because she'd gotten her adrenaline pumping. Teacher Elizabeth had said once that exercise was healthy. She said it could help relieve stress because exercise released pain-killing hormones called "endorphins."

Maybe on the day of the Christmas program, I'll run to the schoolhouse, Rachel thought. *Then I'll have plenty of endorphins and won't feel so nervous.*

Chapter 11

Unexpected News

The sweet smell of sausage cooking on the stove drew Rachel into the kitchen one Monday morning in late November. "I'm so hungry I could eat a whole hog," she told her mother, who was cracking eggs into a bowl. "Will breakfast be ready soon?"

Mom nodded.

Rachel stepped close to the stove and sniffed the sausage links in the iron skillet. "Umm. . .those sure smell *wunderbaar*. Don't you just love the taste of sausage, Mom?"

Mom let out a feeble cry, covered her mouth with her hand, and darted out the back door.

Rachel stared after her mother and shook her head. "Now that's sure strange. I wonder what Mom's problem could be?"

A few minutes later, Jacob entered the kitchen, carrying an armload of kindling. "Mom's on the porch. She said to ask you to watch the sausage cooking on the stove," he said. He dropped wood into the box beside the woodstove they used for heat during the winter months.

"Why do I have to do it? Isn't Mom coming back to finish cooking breakfast?"

"I think she's got a *bauchweh*."

"Mom's got a stomachache?" Rachel asked, feeling sudden concern.

Jacob shrugged. "I think so. She was holding her stomach, and her face looked almost as white as that snow coming down."

Rachel's eyes widened. "It's snowing?"

"Sure is."

Rachel rushed to the window and peeked through the frosty glass. Sure enough, big flakes dropped from the sky like fluffy cotton. "Oh, boy, maybe it will snow so hard we won't have to go to school today," she exclaimed. Then she remembered what Jacob had said about Mom having a stomachache, and her concerns returned. "I hope Mom's not getting the achy bones flu. She hardly ever gets sick."

Jacob nodded and pointed to the stove, where

the sausage sizzled. "You'd better tend to those, don't you think?"

"Jah, sure." Rachel raced over to the stove, flipped the sausage links over with a fork, and turned to Jacob again. "Shouldn't you go back outside and check on Mom? Or do you want to watch the sausage while I see if she's okay?"

Jacob grunted. "I'll check on Mom. If I tried to cook, I'd probably end up burning the sausage." He hurried out the door.

"Sure hope Mom's not sick." Rachel sighed and scrambled the eggs her mother had broken into a bowl. Then she poured them into an empty frying pan near the stove.

Mom returned to the kitchen a few minutes later, but her face looked pale. She walked across the room shakily.

"Jacob says you have a stomachache, and you don't look well, Mom," Rachel said. "Maybe it would be a good idea if you went back to bed."

"No need for that." Mom smiled and shook her head. "What's ailing me is nothing to worry about, daughter. *Sis mir iwwel.*"

Rachel's eyes widened. "You're sick at the stomach?"

"Jah. I felt like I could throw up while I was

fixing breakfast, so I ran outside." Mom pulled out a chair at the table and dropped into it. "I'm in the family way, that's all."

Rachel gasped. She had heard others say "in the family way" and knew it meant that someone was going to have a baby. But she never expected her mother to be in the family way. "Mom, are—are you sure?"

Mom nodded. "I'm quite sure. I've had four bopplin, so I think I know when I'm going to have another."

Rachel shook her head. "But—but Mom, at your age, I—I mean, I thought you were done having babies."

Mom crooked one eyebrow, and her glasses slipped to the end of her nose. "Are you saying I'm too old to have a boppli?"

Rachel flushed with embarrassment. "Sorry, Mom. I didn't mean it to sound that way. I don't think you're old. It's just that. . .well, I'm ten years old. I'm too old to have a baby sister, don't you think?"

"Whether you're too old or not, next summer, you'll be a big sister." Mom chuckled and patted her stomach. "And don't get used to the idea that you might have a baby sister. It could be a boy, you know."

Rachel thought of their neighbor, Anna Miller, who had ten children. One was still a baby. Anna always looked tired and always had so much to do. If Mom had a baby to care for, she'd be tired and busy, too. She probably wouldn't have time for Rachel anymore.

"I've had the morning sickness for a few weeks, but today was the worst." Mom reached for Rachel's hand. "Can I count on you to be my big helper?"

Rachel nodded. Maybe now, Mom and everyone else in the family would see her as a grown-up who should be allowed to do things she couldn't do before.

When Rachel arrived at school that morning, she noticed several boys having a snowball fight. With an enthusiastic yelp, Jacob joined them. Rachel went to find her cousin. She discovered Mary playing on the swings. She sat in the swing beside Mary and began to pump her legs to get the swing moving fast.

"Were you surprised to see the snow this morning?" Mary asked, catching snowflakes on her tongue.

"Jah, but I had an even bigger surprise than that." Rachel grunted. "In fact, it was news I never expected—not in a million years."

"Oh? What?"

"My mamm's going to have a boppli sometime this summer."

Mary's eyes grew wide. "Is that true, or are you teasing?"

"Of course it's true. Do you think I would make something up like that?"

"I—I guess not." Mary stopped swinging and faced Rachel. "You know what this means, don't you?"

"Jah," Rachel said, as she slowed her swing. "It means a lot more work for me. That's what it means."

"I suppose it will. But that's not what I was going to say."

"What then?"

"You'll no longer be the boppli in your family."

Rachel nodded. "That's right, I won't. And when the baby comes, I hope Mom, Pap, and everyone else will stop treating me like I'm a little girl."

"You are still a girl," Mary reminded. "But since the baby will be smaller, maybe your family will treat you like you're more grown up in some ways."

"I hope that's how it goes." Rachel frowned. "I'm worried about Mom."

"How come?"

"She's been feeling sick to her stomach. This morning when she was fixing breakfast, she almost threw up."

Mary slowly shook her head. "Sorry to hear that. Feeling like you could throw up is *baremlich*."

"I know it's terrible," Rachel agreed. "I've never liked being sick. If having a baby means getting sick, it's just one more reason why I'll never get married."

Mary poked Rachel's arm. "You say that, but I bet when you meet the right fellow, you'll change your mind about getting married and becoming a mamm."

"Humph!" Rachel folded her arms. "All the boys I know like to tease and make my life miserable. It's not likely I'll ever marry any of them."

"As my mamm often says, 'One never knows what the future holds.'"

Rachel opened her mouth to reply, but *splat!* A snowball landed on her head.

"All right, who's the *galgedieb* who did that?"

she shouted. A trickle of melting snow dribbled down her nose and onto her chin.

"There's your scoundrel," Mary said, pointing to Orlie Troyer. He stood a few feet away with a guilty look on his face. "He looks like a *nixnutzich* child."

"He *is* a naughty child." Rachel gritted her teeth. "I may have to be Orlie's wife in our Christmas play, but I don't have to put up with this!" She jumped off the swing, packed a handful of snow, and hurled it at him.

The snowball landed on the ground. Orlie doubled over with laughter, which fueled Rachel's anger. She grabbed more snow and started after Orlie. She figured if she got close enough her aim would be better. *Swish!* This time the snowball barely brushed Orlie's jacket.

Orlie snickered. "You missed me! You missed me! So now you gotta kiss me!"

"That's what you think, Orlie Troyer! I'll never kiss you or any other boy!" Rachel started for the schoolhouse. She'd only taken a few steps, when she slipped and fell flat on her face in the snow. She bit her lip to keep from crying.

Laughing, Orlie ambled across the schoolyard and reached for her hand. "Here, let me help you up, little bensel."

Ignoring his offer, Rachel scrambled to her feet and brushed the snow off her clothes. She trudged up the schoolhouse stairs, mumbling, "I am not a silly child. I wish I'd never met Orlie Troyer!"

Chapter 12

A Little Secret

"Stop *rutschich*," Mom said. She turned in her seat at the front of the buggy and shook her finger at Rachel. "You're moving around so much that the whole carriage is shaking."

"I feel naerfich." Rachel stuck a fingernail between her teeth and bit off the end. She wished she could have run to the schoolhouse. But no, Pap insisted she ride in the buggy with the family. Now she would be a nervous wreck all through the program because she hadn't gotten her endorphins working.

Jacob nudged her in the ribs with his bony elbow. "You worry too much, you know that, little bensel?"

"I do not," she said, elbowing him back. "And stop calling me a silly child!"

"You don't have anything to worry about," Pap said from the driver's seat. "You've been in plenty of Christmas programs, and have always done just fine."

"This one's different," Rachel wailed. "I'm playing Jesus' mother."

"Playing the role of Mary and saying a few lines shouldn't be much different than reciting a poem or singing." Henry reached over from the seat behind Rachel where he sat with Grandpa Schrock. He patted Rachel's shoulder.

Grandpa quickly added, "They're right, Rachel. You'll do fine today. You'll see."

Rachel didn't reply. She just folded her arms and stared out the window at the falling snow. Her family didn't understand the real reason for her fears. She knew she'd sit by Orlie the whole time, smelling his garlic breath. She knew he'd be waiting for her to mess up. He'd probably laugh louder than anyone else when she forgot her lines.

Rachel glanced at the small gift on the seat beside her. Last week Lovina had asked the children to draw names for a gift exchange that would take place right after the Christmas program. Rachel had been disappointed to have drawn Orlie's name. She'd decided she would buy him a box of peppermints to freshen his breath. It was too bad he couldn't open it and suck on a couple of mints before the program started.

Rachel squeezed her eyes shut, as a tremor of nervousness shot through her stomach. *Dear God,* she prayed, *if You'll help me get through this program without making a fool of myself, I promise to keep my room clean and do whatever my parents ask.*

When they entered the schoolhouse, Mom commented on the lacy cut-out stars the scholars had put on the windows. Grandpa mentioned the detailed winter scene a couple of the older children had drawn on the blackboard with colored chalk.

Rachel nodded. "We've worked on the decorations for several weeks."

"Everything looks nice," Pap said. "I'm sure this will be one of the best programs yet."

Rachel wasn't so sure about that. She didn't see how her part of the program could be any good.

Other families began to arrive, and soon there was a huge pile of coats, hats, shawls, and outer black bonnets lying on the enclosed front porch floor of the schoolhouse. Inside, adults and children doubled up in the seats. The children who had parts in the program scurried behind the curtain at the front of the room.

Rachel's palms turned sweaty, and her knees began to knock as she listened to children recite their poems and perform short skits. When it was time for the Christmas story to be read from the Bible, Rachel, Orlie, the angels, and the shepherds took their places in front of the curtain.

Rachel sat on a stool near the wooden manger with a faceless doll inside. Orlie took his place beside her, staring at the doll. The angels stood to one side with their arms outstretched. Jacob and the other shepherds knelt in front of the manger. Lovina had said no when Jacob had offered to bring one of Grandpa Yoder's lambs to the program.

Dorothy Kauffman, an eighth-grade girl, read the Christmas story from Luke 2, while Mary, Joseph, the angels, and shepherds remained in place. That was easy. Rachel was good at sitting.

When the scripture had been read, the Bible characters came to action. Phoebe and Mary stepped forward and recited a poem: "We are two little angels who have a story to tell—it's about baby Jesus, whom we know so well. Jesus, God's Son, came to Earth as a little child; He was born in a stable so meek and mild."

The girls stepped back in place. Next the shepherds spoke their lines. "Baby Jesus, so tiny and dear, placed in a manger with animals near," they said in voices loud and clear. "Baby Jesus, the Son of God, was visited by shepherds with staff and rod."

Earlier, Rachel had spotted Pap, Grandpa, Henry, Rudy, and Grandpa Yoder near the back of the room. Mom, Esther, and Grandma Yoder sat in chairs behind some of the desks. Rachel noticed the smiles on their faces. They were pleased that Jacob had done so well.

Next, wearing a big grin, Orlie spoke his lines: "Jesus had a manger bed, with only some straw under His head. Jesus didn't cry or fuss one bit; though a bed made of straw just wasn't fit. Jesus, our Savior, came to Earth; He was born in a stable, such a lowly birth."

Orlie had said his lines perfectly. Rachel noticed that his mother, father, little sisters, and older brothers had smiles on their faces.

Now it was Rachel's turn. She opened her

mouth to speak but couldn't seem to find her voice.

Orlie nudged her arm once, then twice.

Rachel pushed his hand aside and swallowed hard. Still, nothing came from her lips.

"Rachel, what's the matter? You're supposed to say your lines," Orlie whispered, bending near her ear.

Rachel nodded, licked her dry lips, and tried again. "Mary—uh—Mary thanked God with a—" She paused and glanced at the audience. Everyone looked at Rachel with eager expressions, which only made her feel more nervous.

She cleared her throat. Oh, how she wanted to bite off a fingernail, but it wouldn't look right for Jesus' mother to do something like that. So to keep her hands still, Rachel sat on them.

"Go on, Rachel," Orlie prompted quietly. "Say the rest of your lines."

Rachel began again. "Mary—uh—thanked God with a prayer of pays. . .I—I mean, a prayer of plays." Several people snickered. Rachel wished there were hole in the floor so she could crawl into it. Instead, she sat up straight, looked right into the audience and said, "I meant to say,

Mary thanked God with a prayer of praise."

Mom smiled at Rachel, and Pap nodded. Feeling a little more confident, Rachel opened her mouth to say the rest of her lines. Suddenly her mind went blank. What came next? She tried to think, but jumbled thoughts whirled around in her brain like the clothes in Mom's wringer washing machine.

Teacher Lovina, who stood at the side of the room, raised her eyebrows and stared at Rachel. *Thump. Thump. Thump.* She tapped her foot.

She probably thinks I'm a real dummkopp, Rachel thought. *And right now, I feel like a dunce.* The other scholars had done well; she didn't understand why she couldn't do the same.

"Everyone's waiting for you to say the rest of your lines," Orlie whispered.

"I know," she said through clenched teeth.

"Then say them."

"Uh—Mary was blessed in—in so many ways," Rachel began. She paused again, trying to think of what came next, but her mind seemed to be completely empty. She squeezed her fingers into the palms of her sweaty hands. *Think, Rachel, think. What comes next?*

Mom leaned slightly forward with a worried

expression. The rest of Rachel's family shook their heads as if they couldn't believe she'd forgotten her lines.

Suddenly, Orlie bent and placed his hand on the faceless doll's head. "Mary loved God and praised Him from her whole heart," he said with a quick nod. "She was thankful for Jesus right from the start."

Orlie straightened and gave Rachel's shoulder a squeeze. She exhaled a sigh of relief. She could hardly believe he had come to her rescue. Orlie had said the rest of her lines as if he was supposed to have said them.

That was something a good friend would have done, not an enemy. Maybe Orlie wasn't Rachel's enemy after all. Maybe he even liked her just a bit.

Rachel felt guilty for all the things she'd thought and said about him. Now she wished she had bought something better than a box of mints to give Orlie for his Christmas present.

Lovina stepped forward and led the scholars and their parents in several Christmas songs. Then it was time for refreshments and opening gifts.

Rachel waited near Mary while their substitute teacher called off names and handed out the presents. She wished she could find a way to snatch the package that held the box of mints and hide it from Orlie. But that would mean he wouldn't have a gift, which wouldn't seem right, either.

"Rachel Yoder, here's your gift," Lovina announced.

Rachel stepped forward and took the package. She placed it on her desk, tore off the paper, and opened the box. Inside were two glass jars—one filled with peanut butter and the other filled with strawberry jam. She picked up the card inside and read it out loud.

"So you never have to eat
tuna sandwiches again.

Your friend always,
Orlie Troyer."

Tears stung Rachel's eyes. She blinked a couple of times to keep them from spilling onto her cheeks. Orlie thought of her as his friend. He proved that by helping Rachel when she forgot her lines.

"Orlie Troyer, this one's for you," Lovina said, extending Rachel's gift to Orlie.

Rachel wished she had prayed about her situation with Orlie, as Grandpa had suggested. But she had been too busy thinking up ways to get even. Now she wished she could hide. Orlie was already opening the gift. She held her breath as he lifted the box of mints and read the card she'd included. Then he walked up to Rachel and gave her a big grin. "Danki, Rachel. Maybe these mints will take the horrible taste out of my mouth when my mamm gives me garlic for breakfast."

Rachel giggled and lifted the jars of peanut butter and jelly. "I like what you gave me, too."

"Glad to hear it."

Rachel shuffled her feet and fought the urge to bite off a nail. This time she was nervous for a different reason. "I—I was wondering. . ."

"What's that?"

"Why have you been so mean to me since you moved here? Especially since your card says you're my friend."

He looked stunned. "You think I've been mean?"

Rachel nodded. "You've teased and made fun of me. That's being mean, wouldn't you say?"

Orlie's cheeks turned red as a cherry. "I—I

was just trying to get your attention."

"Why?"

The color in his cheeks deepened. "Because I—I like you, Rachel."

Rachel was shocked. She bit her lower lip as she looked away. Boys sure had a funny way of showing they liked a girl.

"Sorry if I made you mad," he whispered.

Rachel touched his arm. "I'm sorry for being mean to you, too."

She pulled her hand quickly away, realizing she'd just touched a boy. "Say, Orlie, I was wondering. . ."

"What's that?"

"When's your birthday?"

"February twenty-fifth. Why do you ask?"

"I might give you one of my painted rocks as a present. Or maybe I'll make a hurry-up cake for your birthday." She giggled. "I have two months to practice, so maybe it won't turn out so bad."

He thumped her on the arm. "Does that mean we're friends?"

"Jah," Rachel said with a nod. Then she whispered, "Just don't tell anyone, okay?"

"No, of course not. It'll be our little secret."

Recipe for Rachel's Hurry-Up Cake

1½ cups cake flour (do not substitute)
2 teaspoons baking powder
1 cup sugar
¼ teaspoon salt
2 eggs
¼ cup softened butter
1 cup milk
1 teaspoon vanilla

Preheat oven to 325 degrees. In a mixing bowl, mix the cake flour with baking powder, sugar, and salt. In a separate bowl, mix the eggs and softened butter. Add the dry ingredients and milk alternately to the egg and butter mixture. Add vanilla and beat hard for 3 minutes. Pour into 2 greased and floured 8-inch layer cake pans and bake for 5 minutes. Raise oven heat to 350 degrees and bake for another 30 minutes. Cool, remove from pans, then frost with strawberry icing.

Strawberry Icing:
4 tablespoons (or more) mashed strawberries
3 cups confectioners (powdered) sugar
⅓ cup softened butter

Blend butter and powdered sugar together in a bowl. Stir in the mashed strawberries, adding enough to make a creamy frosting. Spread on cooled cake.